You've *got* to be kidding.

. . . I turned toward the building.

That's when a whiff of panic blew through me.

It was two weeks before school officially began, and I'd only been to Henry Herbert High School during eighth-grade orientation last spring. And the building was a *lot* bigger than Howard Hoffer Junior High. I had *no idea* where I was going.

But once the snares started playing, I figured it out.

And once I entered the band room, I got whisked through check-in stations like I'd joined the army. I was measured for a uniform, handed checklists, music, a hatbox, and a boxy case that contained something called a mellophone, which I was supposed to play *instead* of my horn. What?!

"You can't march with a French horn," said the blond girl sitting at the instrument table. "Well, you *can*, but barely anyone outside of the U.S. Navy band does. It doesn't make sense."

"No, not playing *my instrument* doesn't make sense," I snapped. What was I supposed to do, start over? How would *that* look on my Shining Birches application?

Other books you may enjoy

Notes from an

Accidental

Band

Geek

Notes from an

Accidental Band Geek

erin dionne

PUFFIN BOOKS
An Imprint of Penguin Group (USA) Inc.

PUFFIN BOOKS
Published by the Penguin Group
Penguin Young Readers Group, 345 Hudson Street, New York, New York 10014, U.S.A.
Penguin Group (Canada), 90 Eglinton Avenue East, Suite 700, Toronto, Ontario, Canada M4P 2Y3
(a division of Pearson Penguin Canada Inc.)
Penguin Books Ltd, 80 Strand, London WC2R 0RL, England
Penguin Ireland, 25 St Stephen's Green, Dublin 2, Ireland (a division of Penguin Books Ltd)
Penguin Group (Australia), 250 Camberwell Road, Camberwell, Victoria 3124, Australia
(a division of Pearson Australia Group Pty Ltd)
Penguin Books India Pvt Ltd, 11 Community Centre,
Panchsheel Park, New Delhi - 110 017, India
Penguin Group (NZ), 67 Apollo Drive, Rosedale, Auckland 0632, New Zealand
(a division of Pearson New Zealand Ltd.)
Penguin Books (South Africa) (Pty) Ltd, 24 Sturdee Avenue,
Rosebank, Johannesburg 2196, South Africa

Penguin Books Ltd, Registered Offices: 80 Strand, London WC2R 0RL, England

First published in the United States of America by Dial Books for Young Readers,
a division of Penguin Young Readers Group, 2011
Published by Puffin Books, a member of Penguin Young Readers Group, 2012

3 5 7 9 10 8 6 4 2

THE LIBRARY OF CONGRESS HAS CATALOGED THE DIAL BOOKS EDITION AS FOLLOWS:
Dionne, Erin, date.
Notes from an accidental band geek / by Erin Dionne.
p. cm.
Summary: French horn virtuoso Elsie Wyatt resents having to join her high school's marching
band playing a mellophone, but finally finds a sense of belonging that transcends the pressure she
has always felt to be as good as her father, principal French horn player in the Boston Symphony
Orchestra.
ISBN: 978-0-8037-3564-4 (hc)
[1. Musicians—Fiction. 2. Marching bands—Fiction. 3. Interpersonal relations—Fiction.
4. High schools—Fiction. 5. Schools—Fiction. 6. Fathers and daughters—Fiction.
7. Family life—Massachusetts—Fiction. 8 Massachusetts—Fiction.]
I. Title
PZ7.D6216 No 2011
[Fic]—dc22   2011001166

Puffin Books ISBN 978-0-14-242247-2

Printed in the United States of America

ALWAYS LEARNING   PEARSON

For Shelagh,
for giving so much to Elsie,
but even more to me.
And for Alisha,
who asked for a marching band book.

Notes from an

1

"Dad, seriously. I can go by myself. I'm not a baby." I grasped the door handle, ready to step out of the car. Dad placed a hand on my other arm, probably trying to slow me down.

"Honey, I know you're not a baby. I just thought you could use some help finding the band room." He sighed. I pushed my head against the headrest and fiddled with the treble clef charm on my necklace.

"I wouldn't have to *find* the band room if I made it to Boston Youth Orchestra auditions last spring," I pointed out. I picked at the button to release the automatic lock. "I know *exactly* where they rehearse."

He steepled his hands on top of the steering wheel and regarded me over his glasses, eyes hard. "Elsie, don't be rude. We've spent all summer discussing this." He gripped the wheel, knuckles white. "The audition schedule hadn't been published when I booked the trip to Austria, and when I called the president to ask for an individual evaluation for you he said they couldn't make exceptions. I can't apologize to you anymore. That's the way it is."

"Yeah, yeah, I know," I muttered. Not looking at him, I clicked the lock button and it popped up and down. Unlock/lock. Unlock/lock. Missing the youth orchestra auditions left the high school marching band as the only musical ensemble that would fit into my fall schedule, so I had to join. "Besides, it's Shining Birches that *really* matters, not the BYO."

Shining Birches is *the* most prestigious summer music camp in the Northeast. I'd audition for it right after Thanksgiving, and one of the application requirements is "ensemble diversity," which meant I had to play in a structured group this fall. Which is why I had to join the marching band.

Getting in to Shining Birches was part of following in my dad's and grandfather's footsteps—both of them went there in high school too. And both of them ended up as principal French horn players for the Boston Symphony Orchestra—exactly what I wanted to do with my life. Why mess with success? All I had to do was take their path.

"Are you sure you want to pursue auditioning this year? Starting high school is going to be a big enough challenge for you, I think."

"What's that supposed to mean?" I snapped. I squeezed the armrest.

"It's just a lot of changes, Elsie. You have a rigorous academic schedule. You're keeping up with your Tuesday/Saturday private lessons. You're joining a new ensemble that also practices twice a week. You're younger than the other kids in your class. Shining Birches is typically for older high school students." He ticked the reasons off on his fingers, but his voice sounded weary, like he was already tired of our fight.

"It wasn't *my* choice to skip kindergarten," I reminded him. He and my mom thought their only child would be bored since I already knew shapes and colors and numbers, but had been worried about me being the youngest in my class ever since. And what was such a big deal about having a busy schedule? I'd been plenty busy in junior high, playing in All-State orchestra, taking lessons, and doing schoolwork. "I can handle this. I *want* to audition for Shining Birches this year. You're the one who always says that musicians need to take every opportunity they can to push themselves and grow, right?" There was nothing he could say to that. He just shook his head.

"I'm going to be late for practice if I don't get going," I added.

"Late for practice"—those were the magic words. He sighed again, and then leaned over and pecked me on the cheek. "Okay. Fine. You win. Go."

Unlock.

I climbed out and grabbed my French horn case, feeling

both heated and victorious. Dad could say all he wanted, but he knew how important Shining Birches was to me—and how important it could be to my career. The Boston Symphony resided there every summer, and when I got in, I'd be exposed to world-class conductors and players. I'd be among the best. *One* of the best. As a freshman!

The car pulled away, avoiding the yellow parking lot speed bumps, and I turned toward the building.

That's when a whiff of panic blew through me.

It was two weeks before school officially began, and I'd only been to Henry Herbert High School during eighth-grade orientation last spring. And the building was a *lot* bigger than Howard Hoffer Junior High. I had *no idea* where I was going.

But once the snares started playing, I figured it out.

And once I entered the band room, I got whisked through check-in stations like I'd joined the army. I was measured for a uniform, handed checklists, music, a hatbox, and a boxy case that contained something called a mellophone, which I was supposed to play *instead* of my horn. What?!

"You can't march with a French horn," said the blond girl sitting at the instrument table. "Well, you *can*, but barely anyone outside of the U.S. Navy band does. It doesn't make sense."

"No, not playing *my instrument* doesn't make sense," I snapped. What was I supposed to do, start over? How would *that* look on my Shining Birches application?

"Chill!" she said, holding up her hands in surrender. "I just give stuff out. Talk to your section leader or the band director about it."

"Fine." I snatched the oversized boxy case and moved on, fuming.

By the time I reached the fifth station, lockers, I was loaded with marching paraphernalia and ready to put everything down and get answers.

"Name?" The guy stretched behind the table wore a blue T-shirt and had a pair of sunglasses perched on top of his head. He had magnetic blue eyes. I gave him my name and instrument—"French horn, but everyone here thinks I'll be playing mellophone"—and he gave me a locker number and combo, plus a smile that'd melt chocolate.

Even annoyed, I couldn't take my eyes off the dimple in his chin.

I thanked him, finally pulling my gaze from his dimple and trying to concentrate on hating the mellophone, then stuck the piece of paper in my pocket and began gathering everything. Again.

As I turned away, the hatbox caught on the side of my shorts. The plastic hasp popped, and with an awkward jerk the bottom of the box swung open. A shiny black hat and plastic-wrapped fuzzy thing fell onto the floor.

"Whoop-whoop!" called the dimple-chinned guy at full volume. "Chicken down! I repeat, chicken down!"

The room went silent.

Everyone froze, eyes on me.

This guy—and his dimple—was suddenly not nearly as cute as he had been.

A hot flush spread across my cheeks, and I bent down to repack the box. Then came the clapping, slow at first, then faster: *Clap. Clap. Clap-clap-clap!*

Awesome. I was the spectacle of check-in. A fresh flame of anger at Dad and his poorly timed trip to Austria (so he could play with the Vienna Symphony, of course) flared in me.

"Cluck! Cluck! Cluck!" Dimple Chin chanted, playing the role of maestro. After a second, everyone else in the room joined him.

"Cluck! Cluck! Cluck!"

I stood there like an idiot, stuff scattered at my feet. Was I supposed to do something?

"Cluck! Cluck! Cluck!" They chanted louder and faster.

"What the . . . ?" Angry and embarrassed, I kept my eyes on the floor and hoped the noise would miraculously stop, 'cause, you know, telepathy totally works.

"You have to cluck like a chicken." The guy whispering in my ear did not belong in marching band—or any orchestral band. A snapshot: streaky green hair. Brown eyes. Lots of metal bits stuck in his face. Skinny. Orange T-shirt and faded basketball shorts. "Then they'll stop."

I had to what?

"Cluck! Cluck! Cluck!"

I didn't move, I didn't cluck. The anger evaporated. Fear scuttled through me like a spider. Lime Head nudged me.

"Do it!"

"No way!" I snapped. *This* was high school? This was marching band?! This was horrifying and non-musical.

"C'mon, it's okay. I'll do it with you," he said. I wanted to throw up. "Seriously, they won't stop unless someone clucks."

I nodded, fear in the pit of my stomach, and he whispered, "On three. One . . . two . . . three!"

"Buck-buck." Mine came out as more of a croak than a cluck, but next to me Mr. Green Hair was going for the chicken imitation hall of fame.

"Buck-buck-buck-ba-gawk!" He tucked his hands up by his armpits, flapped his "wings," and bobbed his head.

"Aww, we've got a chicken chicken!" someone called, pointing at me. I scowled, but inside, I wanted to fall through the floor.

Then, as a group, the returning kids clapped a rhythm and sang as I started collecting my stuff:

"Someone dropped a chicken.

Someone ditched the bird.

Screaming Hellcats to the rescue!

The best marching band ya've heard!"

Clap-clap-clapclap. Clap-clap-clapclap. Clap-clap-clapclap.

"Gooooo, Hellcats!" There was some whooping, and

then they finally went back to what they were doing before my social disaster unfolded.

"Punk," the facially decorated green-haired chicken imitator said.

"Huh?" My head buzzed. Was there something wrong with this kid?

"Punk. That's my name," he responded, as if my cheeks weren't still on fire and my hands weren't sweating. As if I'd asked.

Of course. How original.

"Welcome to the Screaming Hellcats Marching Band," he said.

I wished my father had never heard of Austria.

2

I hoisted my stuff and stepped away from embarrassment ground zero. After giving me his cheery welcome, Punk had drifted away.

Good riddance.

I surveyed the room and caught a glimpse of an alcove behind a set of lockers that jutted from the wall. I beelined for it, hoping to hide there until everyone forgot what I looked like or until practice began.

Unfortunately, I wasn't the only one intent on hiding out. I turned the corner and stopped short, nearly tripping over a clarinet case. Three kids sat in a clump at my feet. They were surrounded by piles of stuff like my own.

Other freshmen.

"Sorry," the one with the clarinet said. He slid his case off to the side, making room for me. "Want to sit?"

Out of options, I just plopped down with them—the clarinet kid, a trumpet player, and . . . oh. Sarah Tracer, who played in the Howard Hoffer Junior High symphonic band with me, was there too. Sarah played trombone and seemed nice, but we hadn't been friends. Her articulation was sloppy. One day, sick of listening to her mushy quarter notes at practice, I told her to pay more attention to the quality of her playing. Her face turned bright pink and she never spoke to me again. Her quarter notes got a little better, though.

"That was rough," the boy with the clarinet case said to me. He was wearing a T-shirt with a picture of Darth Vader on it, captioned "Who's your daddy?" Sarah had a chunky bracelet wrapped around one arm and picked at a spot on the carpet. The trumpet player had on a faded Portland Sea Dogs baseball cap. All of them wore an expression that was a mix of relief and terror—glad that they weren't the one who'd been humiliated publicly, but fearful that it would be them next time.

I had hoped that they hadn't seen what happened.

"Eh," I said. I kept my voice light, like it was no big deal, but sat on my still-shaking hands. In wind ensemble and symphonic band, I always know what to expect. Since I'm a year younger than the kids in my grade, band is usually the place where I feel most comfortable. Not today.

"I heard they do all kinds of stuff like that." Sarah leaned over and spoke up from behind a curtain of straight blond hair. She didn't have a trombone case with her.

Actually, I didn't see *any* instrument near her. Bright red splotches appeared on her cheeks. "My brother was in the pit, and he told me they do that stuff to make the freshmen learn the rules quicker."

What was a pit?

"Not a great teaching method," I muttered, still wounded.

"I learned a lesson from it," the clarinet kid said helpfully. "I'll never drop my hat-chicken." He had a high-pitched, crackly voice—kind of like the way his instrument sounded when played poorly.

"Totally," Sarah agreed. "Not that I have a chicken to drop," she added, then eyed me.

"I thought you played trombone?" I asked.

She shook her head. "Not this year. I'm on color guard." She must have seen the confused expression on my face as well as the clarinet kid's. "We're auxiliary to the band. We spin flags in time to the music to add visual interest to the parade and field shows."

I was surprised that she wasn't playing. I mean, what's the point of being in band if you didn't play an instrument? And why did a band need "visual interest" anyway? Wasn't the point of going to see a band to listen to music? Then again, I'd be spared her inarticulate quarter notes . . .

"Oh. That's cool," was all I could think of to say.

Was having a high school ensemble on my application really worth this? Besides, according to check-in girl,

I wasn't even going to play *my* instrument. As if he knew what I was thinking, the Sea Dogs guy, who hadn't said anything yet, spoke. He had a wide, easy smile.

"What do you guys play?" As if it wasn't obvious?

"Clarinet. I'm Hector."

"Elsie. French horn. But they gave me a mellophone. Whatever that is."

"Jake, trumpet," said the kid who started the questioning. I caught a flash of hazel eyes under the bill of his cap. "I recognize you from All-State last year," he directed at me. "You played an awesome solo in 'The Great Locomotive Chase.'"

"Really?" I blurted, excited. "You remember that?"

He nodded. "Totally. You nailed it. I was on second trumpet."

I got a rush as I remembered the solo, which I'd played in front of an audience made up of people from all over the state. "Measures forty-five through fifty had this tough run, and I really worked hard on getting it right."

"It showed," Jake said. His smile made my toes tingle.

We talked for a minute about All-State—a symphonic band that was made up of the best players from each junior high in Massachusetts—and then everyone said what junior high they'd attended. Hector and his family had just moved to Auburnville from a town north of Boston, so he didn't know anyone. Jake went to middle school on the opposite side of town from Sarah and me. They were nice enough, but clearly not as serious about their playing as I was. Few people are.

I never get tired of playing my instrument, and I can express how I feel through my horn way better than I can using words. Music is going to be my life. Like my dad and grandfather, I'll go to Shining Birches in high school, the New England Conservatory for college, and then audition for a symphony. I'll get to see the country—and the world—and play my horn while I do it. It's the most amazing job ever. But in order to achieve those goals, I know I need to work really hard, starting as a freshman. It'll be like musical boot camp!

Playing an instrument professionally is like playing a sport professionally: There's lots of talented competition for a small number of spots. My dad reminds me of that all the time. "If you fall short, there's always someone else ready to take your chair," he says. "If you want to be successful in this field, you can't forget that." I wouldn't.

"Hey," Hector said, "I was thinking . . . since I don't know anyone at all here, can I hang out with you guys? I mean, after today?"

Jake, Sarah, and I all exchanged glances. It's not like any of us knew one another or were friends or anything, but I guess Hector wanted people to talk to before practice. I'm usually so focused on warming up that I don't socialize before ensemble.

Or outside of ensemble either.

Basically, I go to my classes, do my work, and play my horn—and that's the way I like it. Sitting around, gossiping about boys, checking out nail polish colors . . . all the stuff that the girls in my junior high did just didn't interest me. Any time I spent with other kids was time away from my horn—and someone else, somewhere else, was using that time to get better than me.

"Of course," Jake answered for all of us, sealing our little group.

It's funny, but after we established that, I relaxed. Even though I didn't *intend* on hanging out with anyone, it was nice to know that I could if I wanted. By the time we graduated junior high, I think most of the kids in my grade kind of forgot I existed unless I was holding my horn.

The whole time we were talking, other kids were checking in and the returning students' conversations buzzed in the background.

A sharp whistle sounded over the din.

"Report to sectionals!" the guy who started the whole clucking fiasco called. "Section leaders, take your groups for warm-ups. Ensemble begins in forty minutes!"

We stood, papers rustling and hatboxes bumping our knees (I double-checked the latch on mine).

"High brass!" a guy with a mess of dreadlocks pulled back in a ponytail shouted from the opposite corner of the room. "Outside!"

Five freshmen, including Jake and me, were in the section. All of them carried trumpet cases. Also present? Punk. He carried a horn. Excuse me, a *mellophone*. Maybe I could finally get some answers about this stupid instrument.

Our section leader guided us across the roasting blacktop.

"Excuse me, Steve?" I left Jake and walked at the section leader's elbow, juggling all of my marching gear.

"Hey," he said.

"I play the French horn," I explained patiently. "And I'm quite good at it. Why was I assigned a mellophone?"

Steve cocked his head and grinned at me the way some people grin at small children or tiny dogs—all indulgent and patronizing. "Because French horn bells face the wrong way when you're marching—so all your sound would be lost—and are awkward to carry. Mellos are loud. Think of them as the horn's close cousin." We stopped at the far end of the school parking lot, under the shade of a large oak tree.

"But—" I tried.

"Just try it out," he said to me. Then, to the rest of the group, "Semicircle up, people. Trumpets to my right, mellos on the left." Frustrated, I dropped my stuff at the foot of the tree with the other freshmen, and opened the mysterious mellophone case.

Instead of the graceful curves of my French horn, what I saw was a trumpet on steroids: a dinged and dull forward-facing bell, trumpet-like valves that I'd need to play with my right hand, not left, and a lead pipe that would quite obviously not fit my horn mouthpiece. A "close cousin"? Try *ugly* cousin.

Well, that did it. I couldn't be in marching band. Forget Shining Birches' "ensemble diversity"—this would be career-ending musical suicide.

"Sorry," I said. "But I can't play this instrument." I gestured with it.

"What do you mean?" Steve came over. Everyone else just stared at me.

"Um, I just can't," I said. "My mouthpiece won't work."

Now, if you know anything about brass instruments, you know that a player's mouthpiece is nearly part of their body. I can play any horn that you hand to me, as long as I have my own mouthpiece. And I could probably adjust to this crazy steroid-trumpet-mellophone, even playing right-handed, if I had my own mouthpiece. But having to change the shape of my face—my embouchure—to blow into a new instrument? No way. It'd be like learning all over again. And, scarily, it might mess up the sound I get from my own instrument. Kiss Shining Birches and a life of travel good-bye.

"You need an adaptor," the section leader said. "Didn't they give you one at check-in?" I shook my head. Steve rolled his eyes. "Of course not." Then, to one of the trumpet players, "Yo, Shaka—run in and get a lead pipe adaptor for her horn so we can get going, okay?"

The trumpet player rolled *his* eyes.

"Steve, c'mon—we're all the way across the parking lot. Let the chicken get it herself."

"Five laps if you don't go now," Steve barked. Shaka handed his trumpet to the kid next to him and went.

I took my place at the end of the line and waited for his return, heart sinking. Next to me, Punk smirked.

Chicken.

Great.

3

That first rehearsal? Easily the worst one in my entire life. Even though my section leader, Steve, and the other mellophone players tried to help, the fingerings for every note were different from those on my horn—and I was playing with my opposite hand. So even though I could blow into it once I had the mouthpiece adapter (and make a pretty kickin' sound, I might add), actually *playing*? Forget it.

"You're going to have to write the fingerings under the notes in your music until you get the hang of it," Steve told me. "We all play horn and mellophone too—except for Punk—so you'll learn." Of *course* Punk only played mellophone. Weirdo.

I'd never felt so frustrated behind a musical instrument before. Actually, forget frustration, this was downright betrayal! My confidence, my talent, my musicality, my *me-ness*, all of it deserted me. Even a simple scale was next to impossible—I'd gak every note or get it flat-out wrong. Punk tried to help, whispering the valve numbers to me before we hit each note: "One, three." "Two, three." "Open." But even with that, I'd first try to do the fingering with my left hand, realize I was holding the valves with my right, depress them, and then we'd be on to the next step in the scale.

And so on. Pain City.

How was this torture ever going to help me get into Shining Birches? My aggravation level was sky high.

"Well," Steve said when we were done, "looks like you're going to need a fingering chart."

"Right, genius," I muttered, rolling the tension out of my shoulders.

Who *was* this craptastic player? I felt like a stranger in my own skin. I'd get through today, then go home and quit. There had to be some other wind orchestra in the greater Boston area that had a practice schedule that would work for me. No way was I coming back here tomorrow.

"Let's run through a few basic commands before ensemble. I want high brass to be *the* example for the rest of the band. Freshmen, step out and watch the returning members."

I had no idea what he meant by commands, but I did what he said. At least it didn't involve playing. Jake and I stood next to each other. He gave me a sympathetic smile. I scowled.

"High brass, ah-ten-*hut*!" Steve yelled. I jumped.

So did the upperclassmen. All of a sudden, they went from standing slouched and loose, horns dangling in one hand, relaxed, to a military-straight brigade. Each of them stood with their shoulders back, chin up, horns slightly away from their bodies, shiny bells pointed at the ground, mouthpieces just below chin height, both hands on the instrument.

"Notice their feet," Steve said. He stepped away from his post at the center of the arc and gestured at Shaka. "Toes forty-five degrees apart, heels together. Knees slightly bent. *Not* locked. *Never* lock your knees. And nothing will break their gaze." All of the brass players stared straight ahead, barely blinking. Steve stepped forward and threw a fake punch at Punk's face. Punk didn't even flinch.

Steve explained that this was the command used to bring the band together, to focus and start marching. We'd better get used to it, he said, because we'd be standing at attention a lot. "And it'll cost us points in competition if you break form."

"Since when is making music about earning points?" I grumbled softly, still knotted inside from my failed attempt at the mellophone. This had nothing to do with the hours of practice I'd put in to achieve expertise on my instrument—it had nothing to do with music. The commands were silly rules to a goofy game. *Ensemble variety?* I hated Shining Birches for putting me through this.

"At ease." At this command, the upperclassmen relaxed

into the disjointed bunch that had been goofing around and laughing with one another.

"Think the frosh can execute?" Steve asked them.

"They'd better," Punk responded. "High brass has a rep to maintain."

I caught Jake's eye. He raised an eyebrow at me. It was a "this can't be too hard, right?" look. I half shrugged. Standing still was easy. But just because it was easy didn't mean I wanted to do it. I glanced longingly at my soft case, with my horn snuggled up inside. I was losing precious practice hours—*sitting down* practice hours, on the right instrument—to do this. I toyed with the idea of just walking away, but contrary to what had happened in the band room, making a scene isn't my style.

Steve put us in a line facing the returning members. Jake stood next to me and raised that eyebrow again. In spite of my crabby mood, I smiled.

"Okay, when I call the command, you move on the next beat—just like it's a piece of music. Make the move as a tight snap, as a group. Ready?"

We nodded.

"Ah-ten-*hut*!" Steve called.

I snapped my heels together and stared straight ahead, clutching the mellophone with both hands. The instrument was getting a little heavy. Not as heavy as my horn, but I didn't walk around or stand with my horn. I peered at Jake out of the corner of one eye.

"Eyes forward!" Steve snapped. I jumped, and did what he said.

Steve walked up and down in front of our line, making *tsk-tsk* noises. "You people need help," he said. "Fix this," he said, gesturing to the returning members.

Punk came up behind me.

"Your elbows aren't right," he said, and adjusted them so I was holding the now even heavier mellophone out from my body. He tweaked my feet, showing me how to position them so my toes pointed out a little, and pushed down on my shoulders.

"There. Hold that." He stepped away.

After a few seconds, my lower back started to ache. Sitting down, playing, I have great posture. But when I stand? Mom's always correcting me and says that I slouch.

Steve taught us a few other commands, keeping us at attention between each one. Finally—

"At ease." Steve's voice reached me from the end of the line. I relaxed, muscles aching slightly. Next to me, Jake shook his arms.

"You'll build up during the season," Steve said, joining us. A whistle tweeted in the distance.

"Almost time for ensemble," Steve said. "And I expect you to make me proud. Chicken—don't play. We'll get you a chart."

I gasped. Never in my life had I been told *not* to play.

To fake it. The shock was so overwhelming it overshadowed Steve calling me Chicken.

"We have to do one more thing before we go," Steve said. "Frosh, you need to learn the high brass chant. Upperclassmen, please do the honors."

A trumpet player stepped forward to start them off:

"One-two-three-four!

High brass makes you beg for more!

Screaming Hellcats in your face!

Blowin' the roof off this place!"

Then came a series of grunts, some cheering, and everyone waving their horns. Still stung from the admonishment not to play, I barely paid attention.

"Get to ensemble! Run!" shouted Steve.

Did I mention I only run if chased?

4

Ensemble was just as torturous. For some reason—you'd think I would have figured it out by now—I expected to see chairs set up for practice.

Uh, no.

At least one hundred of us stood, in yet another arc, on the football field. The drummers were behind the instrumentalists, and in front, at the edge of the field, was the "pit" Sarah had mentioned when we were sitting in the band room: two xylophones, a pair of timpani drums, and some other percussion that I didn't recognize. Off to the side, on the soccer field, I could see a group of girls spinning bright colored flags. Well, *some* were spinning—I guessed the freshmen color guard members were the ones doing all the dropping. I spotted Sarah's blond hair and winced as she nearly hit herself in the head with her pole. The color guard equivalent of bad articulation, I thought, and snickered.

The kid with the sunglasses, the one who'd assigned me my locker and started the clucking humiliation, stood in the center of our arc on a podium above the xylophones.

Was *he* the conductor? They let a student conduct a musical group of this size?

"Totally," said Punk. "Students run nearly every part of the band."

Embarrassed and not realizing that I'd spoken out loud, I glued my lips together.

"Ah-ten-*hut!*" The kid called in a loud, deep voice. Immediately, talking stopped and the upperclassmen snapped into position—as did the whole high brass section.

"Saxes! Flutes, clarinets, and low brass—*what* did you do during sectionals? Get these freshmen to attention!"

Upperclassmen in those sections scurried to help, and the ache settled into my lower back and arms. Steve wasn't kidding when he said we'd be spending a lot of time like this.

When we'd been practicing in the parking lot, we'd had the benefit of the shade of the oak tree. Now, exposed, in the middle of the football field, late summer sun was scorching as it approached noon. The bright sun reflected off the metal bleachers, creating a supersized wok. I was thirsty, hot, and grateful for the sunscreen I'd smeared on before leaving the house.

And still standing at attention.

The conductor put us in parade rest, and then called us

to attention again. We did this several times, until I guess he was satisfied with how we looked and moved. Finally, he put us at ease.

"Welcome to the Screaming Hellcats Marching Band!" he yelled. "I'm AJ, your drum major. We have an intense week ahead of us. Freshmen: You will learn how to be proper members of this group. Returning students: You will help the frosh and memorize your music first, so we can get our field show up and running—and maybe have a shot at beating the Minutemen at our first competition this year!" The band whooped and hollered.

He continued his speech, mentioning something about being too small to audition for the Darcy's Thanksgiving parade in New York, but we'd have a great season anyway, blah blah blah. I tuned him out. I was too hot. And the stupid mellophone was conducting heat like it was made of brass. Ha-ha. I wished for a cold drink and a pair of sunglasses.

"Okay, let's do a concert B-flat scale to get going," AJ said. He put us at attention and yelled, "Instruments *up!*" as he raised his hands.

Five years of playing an instrument, plus eight years of attending concerts, did *not* prepare me for what followed. It was a simple note, but the group was so big there was *power* to it. It was *loud.* My breastbone shook. The note filled me up, pushing against my ears and eyes and *at* me, like a wave. No, not a wave—more like an *envelope* of sound, something that wrapped around me from all sides.

In the orchestras and student groups that I'd played in, making music was all about control: controlling how well you blended in with others, paying attention to the markings in the music to add drama to the piece. Not this. Not now. This was about pure, face-blasting sound.

And it was so cool.

Each time the note changed, I got the same feeling all over again.

We played some scales—well, everyone else played. I took Steve's advice and just faked it, keeping one eye on Punk to learn the fingerings, still basking in the raw power of the whole group.

However, standing and holding my instrument for so long started to get to me. I felt a little light-headed, and my ears pounded with a sound that had nothing to do with the percussion. A bead of sweat rolled down my back and hit the top of my shorts. My stomach gurgled. It was lunchtime, but thinking of food made me want to hurl.

More sweat popped up on my forehead and back. The band was playing whole notes, holding each one for eight counts.

Why did my breathing feel funny? I wasn't playing.

A gray cloud appeared at the edges of my vision.

Was it going to rain? That'd be nice.

"Chicken? Chicken!"

"Elsie?"

"You all right?"

"What happened?"

"She locked her knees."

The voices came from far away, and at first I didn't realize that they were talking about me. My head throbbed. What the heck happened?

I opened my eyes and saw a halo of shadowy heads. I shut my eyes. Was I lying down?

"She's awake!" That came from Punk.

"Chicken?" AJ, the drum major, chimed in.

"Stop that! Elsie! You okay?" Mr. Sebastian, the band director, said.

I squinched my eyes, then opened them. Six or eight people hovered over me. I was most definitely lying on my back.

"Wha—what happened?" I croaked. I tried to sit up.

"No, no!" Mr. Sebastian gently pushed me back down. "Stay still. You passed out."

I *what*?

"I told them not to lock their knees!" A very worried Steve, dreads drooping, came into view. "It traps the blood in your lower body. You faint."

"Yeah," I muttered. "I guess you do."

Someone passed Steve a cup of water, and Mr. Sebastian held a hand out to me.

"Let's sit you up. Slowly, okay?"

I nodded as best I could from my lying-down position. I took Mr. Sebastian's outstretched hand, felt someone else's arm wrap around my shoulders, and let them guide me into a sitting position. The world whirled. I closed my eyes.

"Easy, easy," someone—AJ, I think—murmured. "It takes a second."

I opened my eyes and everything steadied. Steve handed me the cup and I took a grateful sip. The water cooled me from the inside out.

And that's when I was finally able to look beyond the little group surrounding me. Every member of the band was sitting facing me. Or where I was, behind this clump of people. My face flushed.

What an impression. After today, I reminded myself, I'll be gone. I won't have to deal with these people again. I won't—

"Can you stand up, honey?" Mr. Sebastian placed a large hand on my back and helped me to my feet.

As soon as I stood, everyone—I mean, *everyone*—started cheering and whooping.

"Yeah, Elsie!!"

"Whoooo!"

And then, over everyone, I heard, "Yeah, Zombie Chicken rises!"

That did it. Shouts of "Zombie Chicken!" rang all over the field.

Mr. Sebastian and Steve guided me to the sidelines. The members smiled and waved as I sat on the bleachers. I tried to ignore them, but Steve nudged me.

"They want to know you're okay," he whispered in my ear.

Startled that they would even care, I blurted, "Really?" This whole group of people, who instigated my clucking disaster and called me Chicken, was cheering to support me? *Really?*

He nodded. I raised my arm in a wave, and a fresh round of cheers began. AJ returned to the podium. Mr. Sebastian pulled a cell phone from his pocket.

"I think we should call your parents, Elsie."

The horror of explaining this to my dad—that I'd fainted while pretending to play an instrument other than my horn—raced through me. I switched from feeling overheated to ice cold.

"Uh, no. No, thank you," I amended. "I'm fine. Really. Maybe I could just . . . sit and watch?" I tried, hoping that would satisfy him.

"Well," he said, brow wrinkled. "It's not exactly school policy—"

"But I'm fine. Steve was right. I locked my knees. It won't happen again," I said hurriedly.

Of course it wouldn't happen again. I'd never step on a football field again for as long as I lived.

5

I let myself in through the kitchen door and plopped the seven zillion tons of brass instruments, papers, and embarrassing memories on the floor next to the bench at our table. Mom hates it when I leave my stuff there, but it's convenient and I really didn't feel like carrying anything an inch farther than I needed to. I was torn between wanting to slither to the floor in exhaustion and filling the largest glass I could find with ice cubes and Diet Coke and *then* slithering to the floor. Option two seemed the way to go.

I grabbed a glass from the dish rack and opened the freezer, basking in the chill. Although I'd had water and sat out for the rest of the morning session at practice, this was the hottest I'd been in a long time—maybe since we'd taken our annual trip to the Berkshires for Dad's summer concert series and enjoyed all of Mahler III during a heat wave four years ago. It's a long, long symphony.

To get through the last movement I had to stick an ice pack down the back of my shirt.

I staggered to the den and flopped on our oversized plaid sofa, icy beverage perched on my stomach. My whole body hurt: back, arms, thighs . . . even my face, which ached from playing and felt shiny and hot from the sun. I'd been at camp for four hours and bailed on the all-band lunch to come home—but since I'd passed out, no one tried to stop me when I left. They expected me back for an afternoon/evening session from two to six. More of that torture? No way. I'd have my dad drop the mellophone off at the band room the next morning and be done with marching *anything*, let alone marching band. Tail between my legs, I'd put aside my Vienna-fueled anger and ask him to help me find a local youth orchestra that would accept me this week. Maybe he could even pull in a few favors to get me a late audition somewhere other than Boston Youth.

Because no matter what, I needed an ensemble for that Shining Birches application.

I lay there for a few more minutes, but the throbbing in my muscles finally motivated me to move. I needed an aspirin.

About to climb the stairs to the second floor, I heard my dad's voice coming from the front of the house. He spends three days a week at a practice studio in Boston, practicing, preparing for his gigs, or giving lessons. I hadn't realized he was around, and as much as I didn't want to have the conversation, I needed to tell him I was home and not going back for the afternoon session.

His voice floated from under the door of my parents' shared office. I stood outside, prepared to knock, when what he was actually saying sunk in:

"She thinks that she can get in, Mike, but I'm not so sure. We've talked about it, but she's adamant about auditioning this year. Maybe I should put a call in to Richard Dinglesby." A pause. "Blind auditions in November." Another pause. "I just don't want her to be disappointed." He quieted, listening to the person on the other end of the phone. Based on the "Mike" reference, I guessed he was talking to his college roommate, who was also a musician.

And talking *about* me. And my Shining Birches audition. And by the sound of it, he completely doubted my ability to do well.

I thought I'd felt queasy on the field, but that was the tiniest wave compared to the tsunami of nausea that crashed through me at his words.

"I just don't think it's the right time for her," Dad finished. "It'd be too much. She's too young and she wasn't able to audition for Boston Youth Orchestra this spring. That's really the proving ground."

That was it. The vomit-y feeling disappeared, replaced in an instant with utter rage. Shining Birches was *the* best program in the Northeast—maybe in the whole country— and he didn't think I could do it. He didn't think I could handle it, and he felt the need to tell everyone he knew, evidently.

And it was his fault that I couldn't audition for Boston Youth!

Well, I'd show him. I would be better than good. I'd be better than he ever was as a kid—I'd be *great*. I'd totally handle all of it—school, marching band, and audition prep—without his help. *And* I'd get in to Shining Birches. Then what would he say?

I stepped away from the door, sure that the heat from my rage would set the wood on fire—or at least melt the ice cubes in my drink. I took the stairs two at a time, taking care not to make too much noise and bring Dad out of the office. I needed to find that aspirin and get back to band camp.

The afternoon was more of the same as the morning: Stand. Play. March. Stand. Play. March. Stand. We got what our section leaders called "band buddies," which is a three-ring binder with a strap on it, so you can wear it like a messenger bag. Inside were pages and pages of our drill—the marching formations we'd learn to make on the field during the show.

Little x's with numbers next to them showed each person's position. I was number forty-eight, and I squinted at the book to find out where I was supposed to stand. After a minute, I spotted the tiny number a couple of spaces off the line marked "45."

Jake couldn't find his number, and Steve was busy helping someone else, so he wandered over to me, band buddy extended.

"Help a section member out?" he said with a grin. He was number forty.

"Sure." I wasn't sure I was qualified to be help to anyone, but he didn't seem to mind. We nearly bumped heads over the top of the drill chart and I pulled back with a nervous laugh.

"There you are." I stabbed at the page. He was also off the forty-five, a few people behind me. With a "Thanks, Chicken!" tossed over his shoulder, he scooted back to the trumpets. Why hadn't he asked one of them for help?

AJ, the drum major, called us to attention, then put us in parade rest to explain how the drill charts worked. Essentially, marching bands divide the entire field into a grid, and at all times you're supposed to know where on the grid you are. You figure that out by counting steps— eight steps between every yard line—and everyone takes the same size stride and starts with their left foot. So before we even set up for drill AJ had the freshmen stand shoulder to shoulder and march the length of the football field, from one goalpost to the other, while yelling, "One-two-three-four-five-six-seven-LINE!" to get us to march properly and in step. We did this *five times*. FIVE!

And the entire time I concentrated harder and yelled louder than anyone else—probably scaring Hector, on my left, and Jake, on my right—ignoring the sweat dripping down my back and my burning arms. Forget asking Dad to help me find a new ensemble.

I wasn't going to quit.

I was going to get in to Shining Birches on my own.

I was going to prove my dad wrong.

6

Over the next week, I attended every band camp session and doubled my practice time at home to learn the hateful mellophone. The fingering chart helped, but playing with the opposite hand really slowed me down. However, the sound I was able to produce was *amazing*. The French horn is made of eighteen feet of coiled brass tubing, and the mellophone uses much less than that. So my lungs, which are used to blowing air over a dozen feet before making a sound, can blast through the mellophone like a brakeless freight train going downhill. Basically, I'm really, really, loud.

And once I figured that out, I blew my brains out. Figuratively speaking. On the last day of band camp, Steve eyed me all during sectionals.

"*Someone's* learning how to toot her new horn," he teased.

"*Someone* better watch out," I tossed back, "because

I will get so good on this, your dreads will go straight." Steve stepped back in mock fear, and the rest of the section *ooh-ed* and laughed at my comment.

I'm glad they thought it was funny, but when I first said it, I didn't mean it to be.

Then, in ensemble that afternoon, AJ shouted to us, "Hey, high brass! It sounds like someone cranked the volume to eleven! Tone it down."

Punk, next to me in the arc, snickered. "Rein in those mighty lungs, Chick-chick." I glowered, but lightened the breath power. I couldn't help it if the rest of the section couldn't keep up. A football stadium is a big space; you'd think we'd be trying to fill it with as much sound as possible—in a musical way, of course.

After practice, Jake came over to me as I was putting my stuff in my locker.

"You sound good, Chicken," he said, staring straight at me.

I ignored his use of my nickname . . . and the prickly feeling in my stomach. I didn't know what to make of Jake's attention. It made me wish my best friend, Alisha, hadn't moved away in seventh grade; I could puzzle this out with her. We'd bonded over brass lessons in elementary school—she was a trombone player—but she'd ditched her instrument in sixth grade and switched to dance. When she grew up, she wanted to be a ballroom dancer on one of those competitive dance TV shows. We compared practice schedules and went to each other's recitals. And when stuff came up, she totally understood when I said, "I can't go, I have to practice." When she moved . . . well, I still had my horn.

Jake also *almost* made me wish that I'd paid attention to those gossipy girls that flooded every bathroom between classes in junior high, sharing lip gloss and boy-stories. Maybe then I'd know how to act in these types of situations.

"Thanks." The locker door swung shut and I spun the combination dial.

"Listen," Jake said, "a bunch of us"—he gestured across the band room, where Hector, Sarah, and some of the other freshmen were standing—"are going to the Chilly Spoon for ice cream before tonight's session. Want to come?"

I didn't, not really. I had to practice my other—real—horn. Because of band camp's long days, I'd only worked on my classical pieces at night. And with an extra rehearsal this evening to run through the field show, I'd lose even more practice time. But I didn't want to seem rude.

"Can't," I said, and shook my head. "Stuff to do."

A bummed-out expression flitted across Jake's face, which made me regret rejecting his invitation. Why was he even asking me?

"I need to practice my horn," I offered as explanation. My hands were starting to sweat. "My other horn, I mean. I have a big audition to prep for."

"That's cool," he said, and brushed his bangs out of his eyes. "What audition?"

I pointed across the room at the colorful poster outside of Mr. Sebastian's office. "Shining Birches."

Jake whistled through his front teeth. "Whoa, that's the big time," he said. "I thought that was for upperclassmen only."

I shrugged, relaxing a tiny bit. Talking about music was easier than talking about other stuff. I had all the answers. "If you're good enough, they'll take you."

He nodded, solemn. "I bet you're right. Have fun practicing." He waited a second, and when I smiled, he jogged back to the group.

My heart tugged a little as I watched them leave.

When I got home, I felt so good about finally nailing the mellophone that I had to let it out before sitting down to hit the horn. Dad was futzing around in the yard and Mom was still at work. So I did what I always do to celebrate when I'm alone: I busted out some Beethoven. I popped the disc of the final movement of the Ninth Symphony— the "Ode to Joy"—on in the den, and, turning the volume up as loud as I dared, stood in the middle of the room, closed my eyes, and pictured the orchestra in front of me:

the strings starting the melody softly, lightly, horns underneath: la-da da-da da-da-da-da . . .

then louder, more insistent, with the addition of the percussion and woodwinds: ba-da da-da, da-da-da-da!

a stormy flurry, before the vocals begin. . . .

I conducted my imaginary orchestra, pointing to each section, bringing them in one at a time, completely absorbed in the music, washed over by the sound and perfection and beauty of the piece.

I really get into my Beethoven.

The vocals culminate in a huge crescendo, there's a beat or two of silence, and the finale builds to a huge, resonant celebration of choral awesomeness. Arms keeping time, I guided my performers through the movement, heart nearly bursting with the emotion. The last note, and— *silence.*

From behind me, applause.

Shocked, I turned to find my dad leaning against the door frame.

"I—uh . . ." I stammered, embarrassed and wondering how much of my performance he'd seen.

He crossed the room and gave me a hug.

"I listen to that when I've had a great day too," was all he said.

It was just what I needed to hear.

That night, after our final band camp session, I dragged myself home, exhausted. School began the next day, and

I could barely muster up the energy to care, let alone be nervous. In some respects, I guess that was good. I mean, although I'd spent a week with upperclassmen and getting a feel for band, I still had no idea what to expect from high school itself. And the ice cream invite that I'd rejected reminded me of one thing: I was starting high school with basically no friends. After Alisha moved, I wasn't the best at keeping in touch, so we drifted apart. And, truthfully, after she left I felt like I didn't *need* any real friends—I spent nearly all of my free time on my horn or going to concerts with my dad, I was super-busy with band and orchestra, and it didn't bother me that I was alone when I wasn't playing my instrument.

There were plenty of kids in the bands I was in, but I didn't think they'd get my obsession with music and practicing like Alisha had. Take Sarah, for instance . . . before the whole articulation incident she'd been really friendly toward me—I think partially because she was one of the only girls in her section too. But she wasn't a great player and it seemed like we wouldn't have much in common.

However, Jake's invitation and the past week made me realize just how alone I was. I'd met lots of people in band camp—some, like Jake and Hector, I could even see getting to know better.

I just didn't know how to make that happen.

7

Later that night, I tore through my closet, trying to figure out what to wear for the first day of school. I'm pretty average-looking: dishwater-blond hair, brown eyes, and I'm short . . . so people think I'm even younger than I actually am. It's so annoying. Mom had taken me clothes shopping, but nothing we'd bought seemed right: The skirts were dressy, it was too hot for jeans, my capris and shorts seemed way too . . . ordinary. Why couldn't dressing for school be more like dressing for concerts? Black skirt, white shirt. Or just a black dress. Fed up, I finally picked an outfit—gray capris, blue-and-white shirt—and went to bed.

Of course, when I woke up I completely changed my mind and started over. The whole time I was getting ready my mom hovered at the door, asking if I needed help or was nervous.

"I'm fine, Mom. Seriously." I was lying through my

teeth, but she didn't need to know that. I twisted my hair and clipped it, hoping that it made me look older . . . although maybe the music note clip that I used was too much?

Mom was stressed about me going to high school—she stressed about nearly everything—but you'd think she'd *act* calm for my sake. When I finally came downstairs, she was waiting, camera ready.

"First-day picture, honey!" she called, blinding me with the flash. I held my hand in front of my face as though blocking the paparazzi.

"Really, Mom?" She'd been doing this little ritual ever since I started preschool: taking photos on the first and last day of school so she could bookend that year's scrapbook with them. The problem? She never made the scrapbooks. About every eight months or so I'd find her clicking through photos saved on our hard drive or rummaging through a shoe box of keepsakes. "I have good *intentions*," she'd mutter, holding up a report card or drawing, "but I never have *time*." She was one of those people with a dozen projects going on at once, all in various stages. I was pretty sure she was more organized at work—I think you had to be, as a bank manager—but she left those skills at the office.

I scarfed some orange juice and a bagel, Mom snapping photos the whole time. Dad came downstairs, jingling car keys in his pocket and whistling "Ode to Joy."

"Congratulations!" he said, and gave me a peck on the cheek. "You look beautiful, honey."

I blushed. "Thanks, Dad. I gotta catch the bus," I said, and slung my backpack and French horn case—dotted with oval airport stickers from the places my dad traveled (plus a scratched-off one from the fateful Vienna trip)—over my shoulder. I had a private lesson after school, and would leave my instrument in my locker in the band room so that when Dad picked me up we could go straight to Mr. Rinaldi's house.

"I'll drive you today," Dad said, smiling. "It's a special occasion."

Did parents drive kids to high school? Would that be weird? But I kind of didn't want to go by myself.

"Okay," I mumbled.

"Have a wonderful day, Elsie," Mom said, squeezing me. I breathed in her mom-smell: the spicy note of her perfume mixed with an undertone of the vinegar and baking soda mixture she cleaned with. For a second, I felt the same way as I had on my first day of first grade, small and scared. I squeezed Mom tight before letting go.

Dad and I walked to the car while Mom waved from the window. After he backed out of the driveway, Dad glanced at me.

"Nervous?" he asked.

I shook my head, in spite of the butterflies flitting around my stomach. "Not really," I lied for the second time that morning. "Being at band camp gave me a pretty good idea of where stuff is."

"That's good." He tilted his head, like he was thinking. "You know, Elsie, there's more to feeling comfortable in high school than just knowing where things are."

I didn't know where this was going, so I didn't say anything, but my heart sped up.

"I want you to watch out for yourself," Dad said. "People might try to take advantage of you."

"*People.*" Oh no—was my dad trying to talk to me about boys? I immediately regretted accepting the ride.

He cleared his throat and went on. "You know, certain . . . ah, factors may make you vulnerable in others' eyes. And I want you to protect yourself. So I thought we could clearly set up some rules for this year."

This was the worst car trip ever. "Look, Dad, I know I'm short and young, and all the other things that worry you, but I'll be fine. Seriously. No one is going to take advantage of me." I glanced at him, then turned to the window, hoping that would end the conversation.

"I appreciate that," he said, in his "I'm going to say this no matter what" dad-voice, "but we're still going to have rules that make us both comfortable. So, I would like to meet any gentlemen friends that you make this year, and you are not allowed to go on dates without my permission." He rushed through the last part.

The butterflies in my stomach morphed into a herd of

elephants. I wanted to crawl into my backpack and hide.

"I know this is awkward, but I want us to be honest with each other," he said.

He had *no idea* how awkward this was.

"And, really, it's in the best interest of your career goals. I mean, you wouldn't want to get distracted before your big audition, right?"

Up until he said that, I was feeling as bad for him as I was for me. But mentioning my audition immediately brought back the sound of his voice telling Mike that he didn't think I could get in to Shining Birches—and my anger. I took a breath.

The high school was in sight. It looked way different than it had during band camp. For most of the week, we had been the largest group of students on campus— yeah, the football team was there, and the peer orientation leaders, but I didn't see them much. Now the front of the school swarmed with people. People who looked much, much older than me. And Dad expected a response from me before I got out of the car. I exhaled.

"No problem, Dad," I forced out, eyes still on the front of the school, fighting churning emotions. "You're right. I'm so busy with my horn I don't have time for that stuff."

He pulled up to the curb.

Before he could say anything else, I rushed a "Thanks!" and escaped from the car, grabbing my horn from the backseat, palms sweating and heart pounding.

"Hey, freshman, is that a toilet bowl on your back?"

I wasn't sure where the voice came from, but I knew exactly who it was directed at:

Me.

An hour later, I stood in the hall while kids rushed to their next class. I was supposed to be going to French, but couldn't find the room. So far, I'd successfully made it to homeroom and algebra without getting lost. But the foreign language department was elusive. I tucked myself up against some lockers while I studied my map and tried not to panic. We only had three minutes between classes, and the seconds passed with every beat of my heart. I was terrified of being late and having to walk in while everyone stared at me. Did everyone else feel this awful?

I frowned. Where *was* the language suite? I was looking for room 322, but it seemed that the numbers on the third floor skipped from 317 to 325. Grrrr!

"Hey Chickie! Zombie Chick!" The voice was loud, and coming from right in front of me. Couldn't this person see that I was concentrating?

Something rattled my map and I nearly hit the ceiling, I jumped so high.

"Easy, there, Chick-chick, or we'll have to call an ambulance this time." I finally glanced at the talker. It was Punk, from the horn line. Regardless of what Dad said, Punk was definitely a "distraction." Especially now. His hair was streaked pink (maybe for the first day of school?), and he'd replaced the safety pins in his ears with paper clips. He saw me staring at them.

"Got bored in homeroom. Checking out HeHe High's floor plan? Where you goin'?"

It took me a second to figure out what HeHe High was.

"French," I responded, chuckling at the joke. "Can't you get an infection from that?" While I was talking, Punk plucked the map from my hands.

"Probably. Follow me."

For a second, I didn't move. I had heard over and over again during band camp about how upperclassmen would give freshmen the wrong directions to classes to make them late, or play stupid pranks on them to embarrass them. Would another band member—especially one from my section—do that?

Punk glanced over his shoulder at me. "You'll be tardy in a minute," he said.

That did it. I decided to follow him and hoped he got me there on time.

We wove through the throngs of students and Punk pushed open a set of doors to a staircase that I hadn't noticed earlier. With his long legs, he took the steps two at a time. I scurried like a rabbit to keep up.

He pushed open another door, led me down a short

hall, and we stopped in front of a classroom decorated with a giant cutout of a beret and the Eiffel Tower.

"*Bonne chance, petit poulet,*" he said, and took off with long strides.

"*Merci!*" I called to his retreating back. I scuttled into the room and took my seat, beating the bell by a heartbeat.

8

After French, I ran into Jake outside of my history class. He waved and smiled as I walked over.

"Are we in the same class?" he asked.

I pointed to room 210. "Mine's in there."

His was next door, but he didn't move. I thought we had maybe two minutes before the late bell, and I wanted to take my seat and get settled before it rang. Cutting it close before French left me feeling discombobulated for the whole period, so much so that when Mlle. Paquette asked me what my favorite color was I responded "*janvier*" (January) instead of "*jaune*" (yellow). Racking up the good first impressions, that's me. At least I didn't faint.

Leaving Jake seemed rude, though. He fiddled with the strap on his backpack. His hair flopped into his eyes as he asked how my first day had been so far.

"It's been okay," was what I said. *I don't want to be late!* was what I *wanted* to say. My hands started sweating. "We should get going." The halls were emptying around us.

"I guess." He shifted. "I think the horn part on 'America' sounded pretty rockin' at rehearsal, don't you?"

I thought back to the band camp dress rehearsal, where the whole group ran through the entire show from beginning to end, playing and marching.

"It needs more work," I said. "The trumpets should be more precise about hitting their notes and the horns aren't articulating clearly."

His face fell.

"I'm sure it'll get better as we move forward," I added, trying to smooth things over. "Look, we really should go."

Jake's hurt expression and mumbled "Bye" stayed with me even after I bolted into class, just ahead of the tardy bell.

Why is it that when I tell the musical truth, no one likes to hear it?

The next afternoon, I sat at home, horn in my lap, playing Bach's Cello Suites. Every time I picked up my instrument—my *real* instrument—I felt like I *belonged*. I didn't have to explain myself, or worry about what I was saying or what other people would think of what I said. My only focus was my sound.

And today I sounded like crud.

"Come *on*!" I muttered to my horn. "We're better than this."

My fingers were rebelling, not pressing the valves as quickly as I wanted them to. I kept gakking on the same phrase over and over, and there was no way I could hit anything higher than a D. It felt as though I was playing my horn from behind a mask. Frustrated, I stopped and cleared my spit valve, then stood, put the horn on the chair behind me, and stretched. Maybe if I shook it out a little I'd feel better.

I took a lap around my poster-covered room, passing all of the classical composers on my walls. I nodded at Beethoven, offering silent appreciation for the fact that he was too deaf to hear my awful playing. Okay, he was dead and on a poster too, but why split hairs?

I sat down and started again. Better. The notes tumbled over one another with ease, like river rocks. My tone was as mellow as the butterscotch I loved on sundaes, and according to the blinking light on my metronome I was right on time.

And then I came to the andante movement. I sped up a little, but there was a run of notes in there—basically, a quick scale—that I just couldn't hit. My fleet fingers may as well have been mittens.

I tried it three times.

"Bah!" I cried, and pulled the instrument away from my mouth and scowled at it. "You sound like *garbage*!"

"Elsie?" Dad's voice came through my bedroom door, followed by a late knock.

I had no idea that he was home! Since I had gotten into honors band in sixth grade, I never practiced with my dad. When I was first learning the horn we played simple etudes and duets together, but now it even stressed me out when he listened to me from somewhere else in the house. After all, he was the first chair of the BSO! I didn't want him to hear my mistakes—just see me onstage, playing well, the same way I saw him. And since this was one of the selections for my Shining Birches audition . . . well, it had to be perfect.

"Uh, yeah?" It's not like I could pretend that it wasn't me, even though I wanted to.

"You need some help?"

I didn't answer right away. I mean, obviously he heard me struggling, and so yes, I did need help—but I didn't want him to be the one to help me. He was probably thinking that this was another sign that I wasn't ready for Shining Birches. It was so embarrassing.

"We can go through it together," he added. "Can I come in?"

I sighed, resigned. "Sure."

My door opened, and there he was, horn in his hand, like he knew I'd invite him. Kind of like a horn-vampire. Uncomfortable, I stood.

"Just let me get another chair." He rested his horn on

my bed—made in 1921, it was a silver Geyer. I bet it cost more than some people spend on their cars.

He returned with a straight-backed chair and a wide smile. After setting it next to my stand, he took his horn into his lap and waited for me. I still stood in the center of the room.

"Let's take a look at this," Dad said. He patted my chair. That caused me to jerk forward and sit down.

"How about we play it together, half-speed?" he said. I nodded, my voice locked inside of me. What if I couldn't do it? What if I made a mistake—again? What would he think? He always said that mistakes revealed a lack of preparedness, and he spent ages listening to recordings of pieces and making notes on his sheet music. "You should know how a piece of music sounds before you play it," he'd told me a thousand times.

Dad readied his horn and glanced at me out of the corner of his eye, from behind his glasses. I raised my instrument to my lips. Dad tapped his foot at the speed that he wanted us to play and counted to four.

"Dum-da-da-dum-da-da..." We played the run slowly, my fingers and mouth working together and getting all the notes right. Then Dad increased the speed slightly. And again, faster. I was still able to keep up, but a light sweat broke out on the back of my neck. Playing with him was weird. It was like I forgot that he was my dad who mows the lawn and accidentally set the grill on fire last summer. All I could think of was his Boston Symphony job—the job I wanted more than anything—my missed youth orchestra audition, and Shining Birches. How would I ever do what he did, be what he is, if I couldn't master this piece? My heart rate increased and I had to gasp to take a breath—right in the middle of the run.

Dad stopped. "You want to make sure that you time your breathing so that—"

But I didn't let him finish.

"I know. I know. I think I got it, okay? Seriously," I added, when the expression on his face read that he didn't believe me at all.

"Elsie, honey, everyone messes up sometimes," he said. "Learning a new piece takes time."

"I know." I crossed and uncrossed my legs, eyes on my music stand, but my brain echoing with the words I'd heard him say on the phone—that I "couldn't handle" Shining Birches. I wanted him to know I could handle this. I *needed* him to know that.

He smiled a thin, forced smile.

"Great, then. I'm glad you're all set." He sat there, not moving. The metronome tock-tock-tocked, counting the beats of silence between us.

I squirmed.

"Thanks for coming in and helping me out," I directed to the music stand. I didn't look at him. After another few tock-tock-tocks from the metronome, he picked up his chair and left, closing the door softly behind him. And I felt like the biggest idiot ever.

Shame washed over me. Why'd he have to be home? Between classes and marching band practice, my private rehearsal time was scarce and my playing was starting to suffer. This little episode was all my father needed to reinforce his theory that Shining Birches was too much for me. I clenched my jaw in frustration as I packed up. Unless I was positive that he was out of the house, the horn would stay in its case.

9

After three days of freshman-only lunchtime orientation sessions—meet your guidance counselor, here are good ways to manage your time/deal with stress (ha!), and an intro to the computer lab and library services—the school finally let us have a regular lunch.

And, after three days of being in high school, I had no idea what to do. In junior high, I ate alone in the band room and practiced after finishing my sandwich. When I'd stopped by this morning to drop off my horn and ask Mr. Sebastian if I could practice at lunch, he told me he had a meeting and the band room would be closed. So I waited for Jake after history, hoping that he'd include me in whatever plans he'd made.

"Lunch?" I said, feeling and sounding stupid. It just came out stiff and formal-y.

"Yes," he said, and slung his backpack over his shoulder. Okay, as vague as my question was, his answer was too. Should I follow him? Did he want me to eat with him? I had to go to my locker and *get* my lunch, plus I didn't want to lug my bag around with me for the whole period, but I didn't know if that's what high schoolers did. So I settled for waiting, mouth closed.

"I've gotta stop by my locker. See you in the lunchroom?" he asked. I nodded, and Jake disappeared into the crowd.

The HeHe caf was not at all like the junior high lunchroom with its round tables and high windows. Instead, picture a mass of students lounging around tables, more noise than a tuning symphony, and a cloud of that thick, fried-food starchy smell. I stood off to one side, clutching my treble clef lunch bag, feeling young, young, young. How was I supposed to find Jake?

And then I heard it: "Buck-buck-ba-gawwk! Buck-buck-ba-gawwk!" To my left, halfway across the room, was a group of band people clustered around a table, waving.

Seriously, did they have to *cluck*?

"Hey, Chick-chick." It was Steve, my section leader.

"I thought this lunch period was only for freshmen and sophomores," I said, plopping my lunch bag on the table. As soon as the words were out of my mouth I realized how snarky they sounded. Steve's a junior.

"Happy to see you too," he snapped. "I have AP chem this year, so to accommodate the lab I have first lunch."

"Oh." I didn't look at him, instead scanning the rest of the table, which had gone quiet since my arrival.

Jake, Sarah, and Hector sat with brown-bag lunches spread out in front of them. A couple of girls from the woodwind section huddled over Diet Cokes and salads, and two of the drummers draped over their chairs like dirty laundry.

"We were just talking about our favorite movies," Sarah said, probably trying to restart the conversation after my snark attack. "Hector was going on and on about *Star Wars*."

"Not the newer ones," he jumped in, leaning over the table. "The originals. Which are actually numbers four, five, and six in the series."

"Did you know that John Williams lifted a lot of the themes in the *Star Wars* score from classical pieces?" I offered.

"Really?" Hector leaned forward in his chair, and Steve and Jake turned to me, interested. Sarah, I noticed, kept her eyes on her sandwich. She'd been cool toward me ever since band camp, like whenever she saw me she thought of the junior high articulation incident. I wasn't sure if she liked me, and I wasn't sure why that bothered me. It hadn't last year.

Now I blushed. "I don't know much about the movies, but John Williams, who wrote the score for them, was the conductor of the Boston Pops for years. Wagner and Holst, and a bunch of other classical composers, inspired him." I hummed a few bars of Holst's piece "Mars: The Bringer of War," then "The Imperial March," Darth Vader's theme in the movies, for them.

"That's so cool!" Hector cried. I blushed deeper, and dug into my sandwich.

Hector and Steve then spent the rest of the period debating whether or not tauntauns could actually keep you alive on Hoth, while Sarah and I listened. Jake would chime in every few minutes with some bizarre and totally wrong comment—like "Didn't Captain Kirk do that?"— and Hector or Steve would throw a napkin at him and shout "That's *Star Trek*!"

Maybe it was because for once I didn't have to worry about practicing or Shining Birches, but I kind of had fun. Even if I didn't say much.

The bell buzzed, ending the period.

"Where're you guys off to?" Steve asked.

"Elsie, Hector, and I have biology," Sarah said. She gave me a tentative smile. Maybe she'd finally gotten over the articulation incident? I hoped so. I didn't think I could eat with them very often if all I had to listen to was *Star Wars* talk.

Jake had math—honors geometry. "I'm a math geek as well as a band geek," he said with a grin as he gathered his stuff. "You know, Jake of all trades, master of none." Everyone else laughed, but inside, I was kind of jealous. I could never make fun of myself like that.

All of us made our way back into the main hall and Jake and Steve split off to go to the science and math wing.

"May the force be with you," Hector said to them.

After the good feeling I got at the table, I hoped it would be with me too.

On Monday, at our next band practice, we lined up on the field to learn how to march in for our field show. You'd think it'd be easy—stand shoulder to shoulder across the "away" team's sideline (amazing how many sports terms you had to learn to be in band), step off together, and walk straight across the field, stopping when you reached your spot.

Unfortunately, it seemed that no one could walk a straight line to save their lives, and since everyone was still double- and triple-checking their spots, it was total chaos.

After the fifth time through, when we *still* couldn't get it, Mr. Sebastian and AJ were nearly apoplectic.

"What is the *matter* with you people?" AJ shouted. "You're not playing, you're *not even holding your instruments*. You're walking! Can't you *walk*?! The Minutemen will *walk away* with our trophy if this is the best you can do!" He jumped up and down on the podium like a toddler throwing a temper tantrum. I couldn't help it; the sight just cracked me up. I laughed. Out loud. We were supposed to be at attention.

"Who thinks this is funny?" AJ shouted. "You think this is *funny*? Oh, it's hysterical that you guys stink so bad! Who laughed?"

My veins went icy, and a crawly sensation danced through my stomach. Uh-oh.

"Spill it," AJ said, "or you'll *all* do laps tonight."

Everyone stood stock-still, holding at attention, barely breathing. A hot flush crept out from my collar to cover my face.

"I'll count to three," AJ barked. "One . . ."

Should I step forward? Raise my hand? Wave? Do nothing? The people around me—Steve and Punk—had to know it was me who laughed. We were standing too close together for them not to. I slid my eyes in Punk's direction. The corner of his mouth twitched. I didn't know what that meant. Did he think it was funny? Was he mad that he might have to run because of me?

"Two . . ."

Oh, whatever. It's marching band. It's not like it's real band or anything.

I tensed my leg to step forward.

Punk did, instead. "Dude, it was me," he called. "You look like you've got freakin' ants in your pants up there. Chill!" He laughed again, like he was making his point.

"You?" Even from where I was standing—about twenty yards away—I could tell that AJ didn't believe Punk. We have totally different laughs. Mine is a lot higher, and Punk's sounds like, well, the way you'd expect a guy with pink hair and safety pins hanging from his ears and nose would laugh—cackly and scratchy.

Punk nodded. My stomach flipped. Why was he doing this for me? Should I stop him? Was he going to be mad at me later? I had no idea what to do or how to react.

AJ cocked his head like a dog.

"Five laps, then," he said. Punk tucked his elbows into his sides and jogged toward the sidelines. As he took off, I swore I heard him utter a soft "Buck-buck-ba-gawk." I caught a snatch of muffled giggles from the woodwinds nearby.

That did not make me feel better.

"The rest of you," AJ said, "back to the line. Let's run this again. And I mean *run*!"

We raced back to where we began and did the drill again. And again. And every time he entered my field of vision all I could focus on was Punk, gangly legs flapping as he loped by. Thankfully, it didn't take him long to run the five laps, and soon he was back in his spot next to me. Of course, as soon as he started jogging in my direction, I realized that having him in line was worse than watching him run. I felt so awkward, I couldn't say anything. I tried to whisper "I'm sorry," to him, but the words stuck in my throat. I kept my eyes on the ground, or locked on AJ, worrying that Punk was mad, stressed that I'd get caught even though Punk took the blame for me, and just feeling like an idiot. Stinking it up on the field didn't help my mood either.

Finally, on our eighth attempt, the marching clicked.

"Eureka!" AJ shouted from his podium. "Why was that so hard?"

A few people muttered answers, but I don't think AJ would have liked what they had to say.

"Grab your instruments. Break into sectionals. Work on 'America.' We'll come back for ensemble in thirty minutes," AJ bellowed.

Immediately we scattered to the sidelines to retrieve our instruments. I dodged the trombones, which were laid out to spell HI! We'd positioned our mellophones bells out, mouthpieces in, making a horn-flower. Of course, I'd stuck mine next to Punk's. He glanced at me.

"Why'd you do that?" I whispered. After being all bottled up while marching, my words came out more angry-sounding than I'd intended. A hurt expression briefly crossed Punk's face.

"Told you. He looked like an idiot. He used to be a horn player and now he's all drum-major-y. It's good for him," he said.

"That's not what I meant."

Punk shrugged.

Steve gave Punk a long look when we lined up for sectionals, and then turned to me.

"I don't know what's going on here, mellos," he snapped, "but I hate having our section singled out. Ten push-ups. *Now!*"

I'd heard that the section leaders sometimes made their sections do push-ups if they got in trouble, but I'd never actually seen it. For a second, anger flared through me. *How dare he?* I didn't want to put my hands on the filthy ground and exercise.

Then I remembered: No one would be doing push-ups if I hadn't laughed in the first place. Great.

I put down my horn and dropped with the rest of my section. Together, we counted off each push-up—led by Punk—while the trumpets just watched.

Ignoring the layers of grime that coated the parking lot, I collapsed—along with everyone else—after the last one.

"Get up!" Steve called. "We've got work to do!"

I forced myself to stand and grab my mellophone—which no longer felt heavy, even after doing push-ups. Was marching band making me stronger? Jake, at the end of the trumpet line, gave me a big smile, then stuck his tongue out. I blushed.

As Steve counted off and I raised my instrument, a series of tiny realizations pattered through me like raindrops:

Playing mellophone was getting easier.
Even though I did stupid things, these people liked me.
Without trying, I was making friends.
And then came one big realization:
I was starting to like marching band.

10

Three weeks into the school year was our first major marching band performance.

Homecoming.

I stood outside of the band room, watching students stream into our football "stadium" (a few rows of bleachers and a parent-staffed snack shack) for the pregame pep rally. We'd march in with the cheerleaders, play a few of our stands tunes (pop songs and crowd-pleasers) while the cheerleaders danced, then take our spot in the bleachers until halftime.

"You ready, Chicken?" Steve tapped me on the shoulder and I turned. "Time to suit up."

"Totally," I said, but my mouth was a little dry. Just nerves—I get hit with them every time I perform. I'm used to it now. My dad gets dry mouth too. He says it's a family trait. Just one more thing we have in common.

Inside the band room, Sarah waved me over. "I

snagged a spot where we can change," she said, point-ing to the alcove where our little group met on the first day of band camp. "The boys evidently are getting evicted." She pointed, and I saw Jake, Punk, Hector, and the rest filing out the door with their uniform bags. "I think they're changing in the gym. Bye, guys!" As she gave them a silly, finger-waggling wave, I got the urge to sneeze.

I am not a dainty sneezer. As I let loose into the crook of my elbow with, as my mom calls it, a roaring "nasal explosion," everyone in a fifteen-foot radius paused to stare at me. Sarah took a step back.

"Epic," the piccolo player behind me murmured. I blushed.

"Let's get our stuff," I said, and my audience went back to what it was doing.

We went downstairs to where the uniforms were stored. A band mom handed me a hanger cloaked by a bright orange zippered plastic garment bag.

Back in our alcove, I unzipped the bag and laid out the parts of my uniform: black polyester suspender pants (sporting a HeHe High orange stripe) with a waist that was chest height, mirror-like black shoes, a military-style orange and black jacket with shiny silver buttons display-ing the HeHe High Hellcats crest on the front. Sarah and I surveyed the landscape of synthetic fashion failure.

"How do we even *do* this?" she said. "I'm not sure I

can squeeze into this." Her color guard outfit was a shiny silver spandex unitard and short blue skirt.

"Yeah, right," I groused. "You, who are about as skinny as your flagpole, will look awesome in that. I have no hope."

I had on a pair of black nylon running pants, and I followed Steve's advice to invest in a pair of form-fitting bike shorts, which I wore underneath. I kicked off my sneakers, whipped the nylon pants off, and stepped into the uniform pants, pulling up the bib-like front as high as it would go— which was somewhere near my armpits. Sarah doubled over laughing.

"They're pants that double as a bra!"

She was right.

"Very funny. Without your skirt, you look like a roll of aluminum foil," I said, and grinned.

Fully dressed, I felt like I should stand straight and not breathe. Which, considering the first rule of marching band—if it's not comfortable, you're doing it right— meant that I probably looked pretty good. I twirled in front of Sarah, who was adjusting her skirt.

"So, how do I look?"

"Oh, simply stunning," she said. "But sadly, you're not the only one wearing that outfit today." I gasped in mock horror, but before I could say anything, AJ's whistle sounded.

"No hats today!" he yelled as the boys returned to the band room. "Two of our sax players forgot theirs, and will be giving us a stirring rendition of 'This Old Man,' reggae-style, before we take the field. Hellcats baseball caps, everyone!"

"Yikes," Sarah said.

"Glad it's not me this time!" I responded. We packed up our street clothes and she left to meet the color guard while I got my instrument out and found my section.

AJ, as always, was true to his word. Before we left the band room, the two sax players—both boys, one freshman, the other a sophomore—did a Bob Marley–inspired "This Old Mon," complete with hilarious dance moves. Thankfully, AJ stopped them after "he played five."

"Let's go!" he called.

We lined up in our marching formation and the drummers tapped quarter notes to lead us through the parking lot and to the football field. Although I'd practiced there dozens of times, filled with people and decorated with banners, it looked like a completely different place. A thrill ran through me.

We formed an arc on the field and ran through some of our stands music—"Build Me Up Buttercup" and "Shipping Up to Boston" were two of the songs—while the cheerleaders danced. The band even hammed it up, throwing in a few spins and horn swings that we'd been practicing in sectionals. The now-familiar power of the group surrounded me, but there was a new sensation . . . what was the word? *Elation*. Like, total, heart-skipping happy funness. I was into it, the rest of the band was into it, the crowd was into it . . . the whole thing was a blast.

Once the football team came on the field we climbed into the bleachers, where, big surprise, we had to stand for the entire game. AJ would write music selections on a whiteboard as the game progressed—different songs for when we had the ball or when the other team did. Next to me, Punk and Steve shouted at or cheered for the players, depending on what was going on. I've never watched a football game in my life, so I had no idea what was happening. Pretty soon, though, I'd figured out that our near-constant playing of "The Imperial March"—our music for when the team was on defense—was bad news. The score and crowd size at halftime reinforced that.

When we took the field, the previously packed bleachers were dotted with spectators. Our team's poor performance gave lots of kids good reason to go home to get ready for the night's homecoming dance early, I guess. Still, I got a little electric shock as the football announcer introduced us over the PA system, and my heart beat extra-hard as we stepped off into the show.

By the end of the game, I'm pretty sure only the band, cheerleaders, and players' families were left in the stands, and I was grateful that my parents hadn't been able to make it. A 56–0 blowout is pretty painful to witness, and even if you have no clue about how to play football, you know that scoring against yourself shouldn't happen once, let alone *twice*. The band's job is to stay supportive of the team, though—at least, that's what AJ kept telling us—and so we had to cheer and clap for them at the end of the game like they'd won.

Our march back to the band room was more like a trudge.

"One down, seven to go," muttered Steve as we packed up our horns. "Hellcats football is necessary for our existence, but the competition in a couple of weeks is where it's at."

I nodded like I knew what he was talking about.

"You going to the dance tonight?" he asked, glancing at me out of the corner of his eye.

"What? Why?" I said, completely caught off guard and embarrassed for some reason. "Uh, no," I stammered. "I've got uh, other plans." Me, go to homecoming? No way. Once people had started talking about it at lunch I never even considered it. "I'll be at Symphony Hall," I added. "The BSO is playing Tchaikovsky."

"Of course," Steve said, nodding solemnly. "How could I forget?" He picked up his uniform bag, leaving me to puzzle over the exchange.

Why did he care whether or not I went to homecoming?

11

One afternoon a couple of weeks later, Sarah met me at my locker before lunch. Since homecoming, she and I had been talking more . . . and I hadn't spent one lunch period eating in the band room.

"So, what are you going as?" she asked, rewrapping a purple scarf around her neck.

"That's pretty," I said, fingering the light fabric. She'd started this funky accessory thing recently—wearing cool clunky jewelry, or a gauzy scarf, or carrying an oversized purse—and reading a lot of fashion magazines. It kind of made me wish I were more into that stuff, but I didn't have the time to devote to it. "What do you mean, going as?"

She pointed to a sign on the wall. "Hel-*lo*! I know you've been out of it, Elsie, but seriously. It's a dance."

Oh. The sign was for a Halloween costume ball.

I shrugged. "Hadn't really thought about going."

"What?! Come on, Chickie. Really?"

"I have practicing to do," I muttered, my standard response to everything. Why waste a Friday night at a dance? I could have a date with Brahms, instead.

"You practice too much," she said, and slammed my locker for me. "Seriously. You are in high school, and you need to get out."

Not according to my dad, I thought. He probably wouldn't even let me go—he'd say I was too young, or give me a hard time about "distractions." He'd probably never even *been* to a dance!

For a second, I missed the relationship I used to have with my dad. He'd give me all kinds of insider info on the drama behind the curtain of the BSO—who was auditioning for other symphonies, what the guest conductors were really like, which sections pulled the best pranks on the violas (everyone's favorite targets, for some reason)—and it made symphony life sound exciting and fun and special, like the members were one big, dramatic family. I wanted to be part of all of it—the specialness, the fun, the excitement, the drama . . . it's why I worked so hard.

But ever since I'd overheard how he really felt about my playing, it was like I couldn't listen to anything else he said—all I heard were the words "She thinks she can get in, but I'm not so sure." Where I'd once wanted to follow in his footsteps and be just like him, lately I felt that I needed to prove myself to him—be better than he thought I was. Be better than everyone thinks I *am*.

Sarah was still waiting for my response. As much as I wanted to stay home and practice—and *needed* to do that—I had to show my dad that I could do it all.

"Okay," I said before I thought about it much longer. "I'm game. Do you have any costume ideas?"

Sarah squeed and clapped her hands, then started prattling about how much fun we were going to have on our walk to the caf. I tried to ignore the growing knot in my stomach.

We put our lunches on the table and Sarah announced, "She's in!"

I said "Huh?" at the same time Jake and Hector said "Cool!"

"We're all going," Sarah said. "You know, as a group. A bunch of the band people."

"Oh, yeah." Sarah's announcement made me feel simultaneously betrayed—for not revealing the "group thing" right away—and shy. What if someone asked to dance with me? What if no one did? Which was the better option, really? The one dance Alisha dragged me to in junior high ended when, while bopping along to some Theo Christmas tune, I slipped in a puddle of spilled punch and sprained my ankle. Putting me with a partner? No way. Spending the evening with Brahms was looking better and better. I huffed, then slumped in my chair while everyone started talking about costumes.

"We should coordinate as a group," Hector said. "You

know, pick a movie or something and all go as characters from it."

"Great idea!" Sarah said. "We could totally be characters from *Dusk*."

"The vampire movie?" Jake asked. Sarah nodded. She'd been obsessed with the *Dusk* vampires since her cousin took her to the movie a couple of weeks ago.

Steve, who'd plunked down his lunch, groaned. "You can't be serious."

"Why?" Sarah pouted.

"Duh! Every girl is going to go as a *Dusk* vampire—it'll be so lame! You guys can come up with something better, especially if the four of you coordinate."

The four of them tossed ideas around like a beach ball at a rock concert.

"The Scooby gang!"

"Charlie Brown!"

"Superheroes!"

"Villains!"

"*Star Wars* characters!" That was from Hector, big surprise.

"What about Muppets?" Jake said. Silence.

"I like the Muppets," I offered.

"Yeah, me too," said Hector. Sarah agreed.

Steve nodded. "Now, that'll be a good one—retro, without being geeky."

We decided that Jake would be Kermit, Hector Fozzie

Bear, Sarah would be Janice, which left me with . . .

"Oh, no way! I am *not* going to be Miss Piggy!" I crossed my arms. "No way, no how."

"Come on, Elsie—you'll be a great Miss Piggy!" Sarah said.

"That is *not* a nice thing to say, Sarah." I scowled at her.

"Well, you have the hair for it, and the attitude," Hector said. That last part, about my attitude, came out very quietly, as though he was afraid I would knock his words back in his face with my fist. Which, given the circumstances, if I could have, I would have.

"Elsie . . . really, it'll be good," Jake said. "We need you to make the costume work."

"Then maybe you should go as the Three Musketeers," I snapped. The bell rang, cutting off any reply. I gathered my books and stood.

Sarah had this exasperated, helpless expression on her face. "Elsie, it's not that big a deal!" she cried.

"Whatever," I said. I didn't bother waiting for them, I just stalked out of the lunchroom.

Inside, I was churning. I didn't want to be seen like Miss Piggy—bossy and rude and self-centered. Even if it was just a stupid Halloween costume. Why couldn't they have all been in agreement that I was the perfect Rowlf the dog? Comments about beauty aside, Rowlf was at least a musician.

I slammed into my seat a couple of minutes before

the tardy bell and waited for Hector and Sarah. They came in wearing identical frowns, hurt emanating from them in waves.

"We didn't mean anything by it," Hector said, leaning across the aisle. "It was a lame idea." Sarah nodded, but didn't say anything, just watched me with a neutral expression.

There was something about her face that made me realize how stupid I was being, getting so twisted over it. It *was* just a Halloween costume.

"No, it's okay," I said, relenting. "I'll do it."

Hector's eyes lit up, but Sarah's stayed calm, like she was waiting to react based on what I said next.

"Really?" Hector squeaked.

I nodded. "Yeah. It's a good idea, and I don't want to wreck it." And wrecking it could mean eating lunch with my horn—which, I was surprised to find out, didn't hold much appeal anymore—instead of in the caf.

Some warmth crept back into Sarah's eyes.

"Cool," she said, and nodded like she was over the whole thing. The bell rang, and Mr. O'Malley started taking attendance. He told us to review the homework questions with a partner or small group. Sarah bent to get her work out, the delicate ends of her scarf falling into her bag. It gave me an idea.

"Maybe you can help me with my costume?" I asked, shy.

"Sure," Sarah said, voice warmer. "I'll talk to my mom.

You can probably come over on our next non-band weekend."

Hector cleared his throat. "I think we'll all need help," he said.

Sarah nodded. "No problem. I'll get supplies—"

"If I don't hear cellular structure talk coming from *every* group, there'll be a pop quiz," Mr. O'Malley called. "And I guarantee you it won't be multiple choice."

We were all business after that. Inside, I knew I'd dodged more than a test, though.

That afternoon, tired and drained, I could barely focus on my private horn lesson. Mr. Rinaldi had to stop me twice for silly mistakes, something he'd rarely had to do in the three years I'd been working with him.

"Where's my star player today?" he asked, peering at me over the tops of his glasses, bushy eyebrows raised in a question mark.

I shook my head, feeling more like a chicken than a star, and settled my horn in my lap. "I'm not sure," I admitted. "Just tired." I yawned.

"Well," he said with a smile, "let's try something peppier, to wake you up." He paged through the sheet music on the stand and found a light duet that was not part of my audition packet.

"But that's not for Shining Birches," I protested.

"Just because it's not one of your audition pieces doesn't mean we can't play it," he responded. "As a matter of fact, playing something with no ties to the audition is probably a good idea. It'll clear your head." He tapped his foot to set the tempo of the piece.

With everything that had been going on lately—learning the mellophone and marching band, worrying about Shining Birches, settling into high school classes, and maybe making new friends—I couldn't remember the last time my head was anything but packed.

I counted the beats with Mr. Rinaldi, then raised the horn to my lips, hoping for clarity.

I followed his lead on the duet, letting the notes rise and fall, harmonize and separate, trying to stay as focused as possible on the music and leave the rest of my life behind. I tried, but couldn't find that place where I stop playing and just start *feeling* the music. My horn and I were disconnected today, and there was nothing else I could do about it.

We held the last note for an extra beat, then Mr. Rinaldi put his horn down and studied me.

"Did that help?"

"Absolutely," I answered, hoping he was convinced by my smile and didn't look in my eyes.

12

"I wish your father wouldn't hide his peas under his mashed potatoes. I always find them." Mom scraped the remnants of Dad's dinner down the garbage disposal and passed me the plate to load into the dishwasher.

"But you never say anything while he does it," I pointed out. She'd been forcing green vegetables on my dad ever since they got married. "So he thinks he's getting away with it."

"True," Mom mused. "I always think about it at the beginning of dinner, but by the time we're eating I've forgotten." She handed me the last of the silverware and I plunked it into the basket. "It's nice to get you standing still," she added.

I knew what she meant. Between band practice, classes, and squeezing in my Shining Birches audition prep— which was still not going well—I was rarely in one place for long. Lately, I'd taken to staying after band to play my horn, which made for a long night of homework later. I just nodded.

"You look so tired," Mom said.

I shrugged. I didn't want to think about it too much. I just needed to deal. "I'm fine."

Mom slung a dish towel over my shoulder and started washing pots and pans. I leaned against the counter, drying lids.

"I know you're fine, Elsie, but I worry. You're young for all of this pressure, and I wish I were home more to help you with it."

How many times did my parents need to remind me how young I was? Or that I needed help managing my life?

"I can *handle* it, Mom," I snapped. I clanged the lid I'd been drying on the counter harder than I meant to. The sound rang through the kitchen. "I have work to do," I muttered, leaving.

Upstairs, I dumped my backpack onto my bed and stared at the pile of folders, textbooks, and assignment sheets covering my comforter. I had a lab report to write up, chapters to read in *Emma* for English, history questions, math problems, and French verbs to conjugate. And I had to get as much done as possible before Saturday, which was our first field show and parade competition. Forget what I'd told my mom, high school was seriously so much *work*. I sorted through the stack, trying to decide what to do first. Nothing appealed. I hated to admit it, but Mom was right. I was wiped out, and really wanted a nap. I yawned, and glanced at the clock: 7:30. If I lay down for a half hour, I reasoned, I'd still have plenty of time to work on what was due tomorrow. I moved the pile of school materials to one side and curled up on my bed with my "Eat-Sleep-French horn" pillow.

What felt like a second later, a knock sounded at my bedroom door.

"Huh?" I muttered. The door opened.

"Honey, it's late—" My mom stopped.

I sat up, groggy.

"I was coming in to tell you that you should get to bed," she said.

"Bed?" Sleep fuzz clouded my head. "I was napping."

"It's after eleven," my mom said, a furrow appearing in her forehead. "I thought you were doing homework."

"Eleven?!" Shock reverberated through me. Had I really been asleep that long? I stared at my bedside clock, trying to make sense of what happened. I'd put my head on the pillow at 7:30; how had I lost nearly four hours?

"I'm going to bed," my mom said. "And you should too." She came in and gave me a kiss, but I caught the worried look on her face. Fear crawled around in my stomach. How was I going to get anything done for tomorrow?

"Yep," I said, faking calmness. "Guess I fell asleep while I was reading." I picked up *Emma*—which was so far away from my hands that I would have had to toss it to the end of the bed while I "fell asleep" reading it—and gestured at my mother with it.

"Okay, then," she said, and closed the door behind her.

After changing into my "I'll be Bach" T-shirt and fuzzy yellow pj pants, and brushing my teeth, I felt more together. I organized my assignments into the Must Complete Tonight pile and the Can Wait pile. Must-dos: math problems, history questions, start lab report. I moved off my bed and sat on the floor to attack algebra.

An hour and a half later, I could barely keep my eyes open and it looked as though a first grader wrote my history assignment. I rubbed my face.

Downstairs, the front door opened. Dad was home.

Crud! I hoped he hadn't seen my light. The last thing I needed were questions from him—or, I realized a second later—more questions from my mom when he told her that I'd been up. I swept the books into a pile and hopped into bed, clicking the light off.

A light tapping came at my door. I ignored it, pulling the covers over my head.

"Elsie?" The door opened a crack. I made my breathing slow and steady.

Dad stood there and I tried not to move. After a second came a whispered "Love you, pumpkin," then the door clicked closed. The whistled chorus of "Ode to Joy" floated behind him. A bittersweet zap hit my heart, and my eyes filled with tears that I didn't let fall.

My alarm went off what felt like two seconds later. I slapped the clock radio snooze button at least three times and finally dragged myself out of bed when I heard my mom coming up to check on me. Getting ready and out the door was awful—even after a purposely-chilly shower, I was still groggy and sluggish and my mom kept giving me looks like she wanted to say something, but didn't. I wished my parents would allow me to drink coffee.

By the time the bus arrived at HeHe, I'd woken up a little. The crisp October air and bright sunshine had helped. I made my way to my locker.

"Hey, Elsie!" Hector waved at me from across the hall and came to lean against the locker bank next to mine. "Yikes! A little rough around the edges?" he asked once he got close enough to get a good look at me—hair a wreck, permanent scowl, and bloodshot eyes.

"Gee, thanks," I muttered, not trying to hide the sarcasm dripping from my voice. "Do those observations win you many friends?"

Hector backed up a step or two. Ouch. Maybe that was too harsh.

"I'm really tired," I tried again. I crammed a few books into my locker and grabbed my notebook.

"I guess," Hector said, frowning. "See you at lunch." The first bell rang and he disappeared into the crowd. Great. Now I felt bad about my behavior on top of feeling gross in general. This was turning out to be a winner of a Wednesday. I trudged toward homeroom.

Wednesday.

Wednesday. What was it that made Wednesday stick in my head?

Midstride, I froze. And barely heard the snide "Freshman!" snarl from a sophomore girl who almost fell over me.

Today was Wednesday. Our first field show competition was Saturday, and we had a dress run-through this afternoon. I was supposed to bring my hat! Ice slid through my veins. What band-o-rific punishment would I be given? Running laps wearing a cape? Clucking the 1812 Overture?

Around me, the halls were emptying. Hatless or not, if I wanted to make it to homeroom before the late bell, I'd have to sprint.

At lunch, I rushed to our table, stack of unfinished homework under my arm and stomach churning from worrying all morning. I wanted to beat Steve there so I could discuss my problem with Jake, Hector, and Sarah.

I tossed my lunch bag on the table and plopped the papers beside it. Steve hadn't arrived yet.

"Elsie!" Hector cried. "Help me out: that song from the movie *2001: A Space Odyssey*—bah-dah-BA-DAH!—"

"Richard Strauss. It's called 'Thus Spoke Zarathustra,' but that's the name of the whole piece. The section they used in the movie is actually a movement called 'Sunrise.' The Pops played it a couple of years ago." I waved my hand at Hector's gaping mouth. "But that doesn't matter. I forgot my hat."

All three of them shook their heads.

"Dude!" Jake said. "Elsie! We need them for run-through."

"I *know* that," I snapped.

"Steve is going to kill you," Sarah said.

"I know that too. That's why I'm telling you before he gets here. Help me out!" Desperate, anyone?

The others exchanged helpless looks.

"I don't know what we can do," Hector said. Today he was wearing a *Star Wars* shirt that read: "I'm not lazy, I just have a bad motivator" around a picture of a robot. I didn't get it. He added, "It's not like any of us have an extra shako hidden in our lunch bags or anything."

Okay, I deserved that for my snarky comment this morning. I leaned back in my chair and closed my eyes, the sound from hundreds of conversations bouncing off the caf's walls.

"Can you call someone and have it dropped off?"

Sarah's voice rose out of the din. My dad *was* probably still home. His quintet rehearsed on Wednesdays, but I think they met in late afternoon. He'd probably grumble about having to come by the high school, but at least I wouldn't be running laps or making farm noises for the marching band.

I opened my eyes and sat straighter. "Yeah, I'll call my dad."

"Steve will never have to know," Sarah said, triumphant.

"Steve would never have to know what?" His deep voice was right behind me.

Sarah turned pink.

"Ba-daaa . . . BA-DAH!" sang Hector. I glared at him.

"Nothing," Jake said. "It's cool." He slid his chair over so Steve could sit.

For the rest of lunch I worked on the lab report I was supposed to finish the night before while Steve helped Jake with some big extra-credit math problem. Hector and Sarah made supply lists for our Halloween dance costumes. Just before the bell rang, Jake brought me to the far side of the caf so I could use his cell phone. His hair flopped over his eyes as he showed me how to unlock the key pad, and my heart did a funny stop-start.

The phone purred in my ear until Dad picked up and I explained that, no, I was not sick or anything—I just needed my band hat.

"You need to be responsible for your own belongings," my dad said in his lecture-voice. "A professional musician is always prepared."

I gritted my teeth against the shame his words delivered. It's not like I forgot something every week. And, seriously, what did my band hat have to do with being a professional musician?! "I know, Dad. I just left in a rush this morning and forgot. It won't happen again." I took a deep breath, stressed. "The bell's going to ring and I need to go to class."

He sighed. "Fine, Elsie. I'll drop it off in the front office this afternoon, on my way to rehearsal. Last time though, okay?"

Only time, I wanted to add, but I thanked him and clicked the phone off. Our conversation left me feeling like a deflated tire. Before this year, Dad and I had so much in common, so much to talk about; everything was easy between us. But now it was as though every time we spoke, someone was saying the wrong thing or hearing different words. I sighed.

Jake, who'd nicely stepped away to give me some privacy, slipped the phone back in his pocket and raised an eyebrow at me.

"He's going to bring it."

"Cool." Jake turned away, then back, like he wanted to say something.

"What?" I said, immediately regretting the harsh way

the word came out. What was wrong with my mouth today?

"Nothing," Jake said, eyes to the floor. Not before I saw the hurt in them, though. "Glad it's okay."

That wasn't what he wanted to say, and I knew it, but the moment was gone.

13

At the end of the day, I stopped by the front office and picked up the ugly plastic shako box. For our dress rehearsal we were supposed to wear our hats—not full uniforms—so AJ and Mr. Sebastian could more clearly see our formations during the drill. Plus, it'd get us freshmen used to playing with the hats' goofy chin chain that draped just below our lower lips.

We ran through the field show a few times, then were called to the sidelines and told to suit up. I opened my hatbox, careful not to let anything spill, and removed the heavy headwear. No plume-chicken needed today.

I balanced it on my head and felt a tap on my shoulder. Punk.

"You need to straighten it, Chicken," he said. He grabbed both sides of the hat and adjusted it until it felt like it was going to come off. "If you're wearing it right, the balance feels funny. It takes some getting used to."

"No kidding," I said. How was I going to play like this? The other events we'd done at school since homecoming consisted of us wearing our band T-shirts and baseball caps, so we hadn't had to get decked out yet.

Prep time over, AJ called us back to opening set and put us at attention. The hat wobbled on my head as I brought the horn up. The brim was low over my eyes, causing me to overshoot my spots. Based on AJ's shouting, others were having just as much trouble as I was. Amazing how the simple addition of a piece of ugly headwear could mess up everything you'd been working on for nearly two months.

"Watch it!" came Punk's voice. I narrowly missed crashing into the clarinetist in front of Hector who I was used to seeing a lot sooner, thanks to Mr. Hat. That put me off step, and I had to do a little skip-hop to catch up and get back into alignment with my group. I heard Hector snicker. This was like starting all over again. Frustration rose in me, and I fought it, focusing on staying in step, playing, and hat balancing.

We finished the show and stood in our final set: a "company front"—standing shoulder to shoulder from thirty yard line to thirty yard line. It seemed like every freshman was at least a step out of their spot. We looked more like a gap-toothed smile than a straight line.

"Well," AJ called from the podium, "that was a horror show. Reset, and let's do it again!"

Thursday and Friday slipped by, and I managed to get mostly caught up on my homework. Steve assured me that I'd have some downtime between the parade and field show competition on Saturday afternoon, so if I really needed to, I could bring school stuff.

"However," he cautioned, "there'll be a zillion distractions and you probably won't get much done."

Distractions, I could handle. And although I felt tingles of excitement surrounding the field show competition, I was downright panicked over not being able to practice for Shining Birches for two whole days. The audition was six weeks away! But although my playing chops needed a night off before the show to ensure their full strength for Saturday, I couldn't help but wonder if taking time away from my French horn meant a competitor would win my spot at Shining Birches. Tension knotted my back and shoulders.

And it made me really pleasant too.

"Stupid shoes!" I snarled as I kicked Dad's concert dress shoes away from the door. I held about thirty gazillion pounds of band stuff—shoes, hat, mellophone, music, and a backpack full of field show competition must-haves—and was waiting for Steve to pick me up so we could meet the band bus at the high school.

My mother called a sharp, "Elsie Kate! Do *not* speak in that tone!" from the other room.

I left, trying really hard not to slam the door, which opened not two seconds after I stepped outside. Dad.

"Your mother said someone is going to pick you up?" I stared down our street, not meeting his eyes. What was this about?

"My section leader. Steve. He's going to drive me to the band room, so we can catch the bus to the competition."

"Remember our conversation from the first day of school?" my dad asked. At his solemn tone, I turned. Part of me expected to see a smirk or smile on his face, but a larger part knew it wouldn't be there. The larger part was right. He was serious.

"It's my section leader, Dad. It's *daytime*. We're going to school. With other people. To take a bus to a band competition." Did he think I was going to a party? My dad had never cared about this stuff before. We were strangers to each other. Where did the dad go who argued Beethoven vs. Wagner with me?

"I've never met this boy."

A little blue car turned onto our street. It had to be Steve. No one else in our neighborhood drove a tiny car like that. My heart thudded in my chest. I didn't want Dad asking Steve a ton of questions. The thought of that embarrassed me almost as much as the chicken-dropping incident. Would Steve call me "Baby Chick" if Dad got too involved? Or something even worse?

It's only band, I thought, trying to keep calm. Why was

Dad rattling me? I didn't like-like Steve—no way!—so what was the big deal? My dad needed to chill out.

Steve's car slowed to a stop in front of our house. I could hear marching band music pouring from his speakers and saw a figure sitting in the passenger seat. I was pretty sure it was Jake. Great. *Two* boys. Dad will love this.

I reached down for the mellophone case, but Dad already had the handle. "Let me help you with that," he said. A total excuse to walk me to the car.

"Sure," I muttered.

Steve popped out of the car when he noticed that both of us were moving toward him. "Mr. Wyatt," he said, holding out his hand. Dad shook it. "It's a pleasure to see you, sir. I mean, I've been watching you at the BSO for years, but it's nice to meet you in person."

The fire in my face would melt my bell. Dad immediately morphed from scowly face to professional horn face, but that almost made it worse. He told Steve the story about the night James Levine fell off the stage while conducting while stashing the mellophone case in Steve's trunk. It closed with a clunk.

"Break a leg," Dad said.

Steve thanked him. I exhaled. Apparently, Dad hadn't noticed Jake in the front seat.

"And drive carefully, young man," Dad said. He reached for Steve's hand. "You're carrying my precious cargo."

So much for relief. My face flamed.

"Dad, we're going to be late if we don't leave." The embarrassment-o-meter was sky high. I had to get him to stop. Luckily, one thing my dad is, is never late for a rehearsal or performance. Barbeques and family parties? Those are another story. "Mr. Sebastian says the bus leaves promptly at eight."

"Nice to meet you, sir," Steve said.

"Take care of her," Dad replied. I nearly dove into the car as soon as the two of them separated. Could he have made me sound like any more of a baby?

"What was that about?" Jake asked from the front.

"Distractions," I muttered.

14

If I thought the first day of band camp was chaotic, it was nothing compared to competition day. Band members packed instruments for transport, the color guard practiced choreography and spins in all corners, and others were running around with some purpose I couldn't figure out. I gaped. So did Jake.

"Welcome to crazy," Steve said. We followed him in and plunked our gear down in a place where it was least likely to get trampled, then huddled with Hector, much as we had on the first day of band camp, and watched Sarah practice her spins—she wasn't dropping her flag anymore, and had great articulation. The percussionists packed their drums into big cases while the sousaphone players unscrewed their bells and the band moms grabbed people who had uniform problems. Jake nudged me and pointed to a big note on the whiteboard:

DID YOU REMEMBER YOUR:
SHOES
HAT
INSTRUMENT
SOCKS?
DON'T FORGET—ALL FACIAL JEWELRY AND
EARRINGS MUST BE REMOVED FOR PARADE
INSPECTION!

Underneath that last part, someone added: THIS
MEANS YOU, PUNK!

I laughed. In spite of the activity and busyness, I finally
started to relax. It's here, I thought. My first competition.
It felt different from the umpteen zillion concerts and
shows I'd played in before, and I couldn't wait to see what
it was like when we got to the stadium. We'd be competing
against six other bands, but thirty would be performing,
total.

"The buses are here!" I'm not sure where the shout
originated, but soon others picked it up and it ricocheted
around the room. Then the chant began:

"Hua! Hua! One-two-three!
Hellcats movin'—get ready!
We bring it bad,
We bring it loud,
Screamin' Hellcats . . .
We are proud!"

Our section leaders had told us the bus protocol and that the freshmen would have to load the equipment truck, supervised by the drum line.

After sweating with Hector—who was wearing a gray *Star Wars* Cantina Band T-shirt to mark the occasion—as we maneuvered the boxed-up marimba (kind of like a big xylophone on wheels, only with pedals like a piano) onto a lift on the outside of the truck, we grabbed our stuff and waited at the front of the band room for Sarah and Jake. They came out a few seconds later, Sarah muttering something about having to load the number five bass drum (our largest) by herself.

Jake led us onto the last bus in the line, where the four of us snagged the front two seats.

This is nothing like orchestra, I thought. In the other ensembles in which I'd performed, the audience came to us. We didn't have to lug all of our stuff—we just showed up in "concert dress" (either white top and black skirt or pants, or black dress) and ready to play. We hadn't even started the performance part of the day and I'd already done more heavy lifting and organizing for marching band than I ever did in orchestra! But in marching band, we didn't have to jockey for chair position . . . and there was more than applause at stake tonight: A big, shiny trophy was up for grabs.

It's funny—since I never played sports when I was a little kid (it was hard to get me to come out from behind a music stand, even in elementary school), and music was less about competing with others and more about me competing with myself to be the best player I could, I never thought much about winning and losing. But the idea that the musical group I was a part of would be judged against other bands? Well, that sparked a new competitive streak in me. All I wanted was to win that trophy—to be part of the best group on the field and have everyone know it.

Sarah slid into the seat next to me. She'd stayed lukewarm toward me since I'd flipped out over being Miss Piggy, so I hoped this was a good sign. She gestured to the history book propped on my knees and asked if I was going to do the reading.

"If I can stay awake long enough," I said. As if on cue, I yawned so big my jaw cracked. She giggled.

"Chicken, cock-a-doodle-do!" someone called, and jostled my shoulder. The bus was mostly empty and Steve was peering into my seat. I glared at him. Where was Sarah? Why hadn't she woken me up? Was she still mad at me after all?

"Get your stuff and get suited up! We're due in warm-ups in twenty minutes!" He leaped off the bus.

I grabbed my backpack of supplies and pulled the mellophone case out of the overhead rack. When I stepped off the bus into the crisp October sunshine, my hands tingled with adrenaline. My first competition!

The girls' changing area was between buses one and

two. A band mom handed me my uniform bag and I found Sarah, who'd spread her towel on a grassy patch. But once I saw her, I didn't know if I should approach her or not. What should I say about the bus? Why did I care?

"Hey! Sleeping Chicken!" She waved and called me over. "You were so out of it that I couldn't bring myself to wake you up."

I smiled, more relieved than I expected to be. She made room next to her stuff, and I spread my towel and got my uniform out. Around us, other girls from band and color guard were getting decked out in their polyester finest, giggling or complaining over each piece of band-tastic clothing.

As we changed, Sarah chatted about a fashion design elective that she wanted to take in the spring. She didn't leave me much time to respond—I wouldn't have really known what to say anyway—so I just nodded and smiled as she prattled. Her enthusiasm reminded me of when Alisha talked about dance, which I hadn't realized how much I'd missed. It was nice to listen to someone else so into their "thing," even if it wasn't music-related.

It was nice to have someone else to listen *to*, too.

AJ's whistle tweeted over everyone's chatter. Time to line up. Sarah headed off with the rest of the color guard. I grabbed my hat, stuck the chicken-plume in the slot in the center front of it, and raced to the warm-up area.

In uniform, we were intimidating. Thanks to the

cut of the jackets and pants, it was nearly impossible to distinguish who was male or female, let alone identify individuals. We stood in our warm-up arc, and the serious and focused expressions on everyone's faces reminded me of how classical musicians look before a performance. Even Punk, who I almost didn't recognize without the nuts and bolts in his face, seemed intense. AJ warmed us up, then gave us basic instructions about the inspection, parade, group photos, and the downtime before the field show performance. By the time he finished explaining everything, butterflies had taken up residence in my stomach.

"Remember," AJ cautioned, "at inspection *everything* counts! A speck of lint on your pants will get points knocked off. A crooked hat—we lose a point. Earrings? Nose rings? Deductions. Not standing at attention properly? Instrument dirty? *Mega* points off. And they identify you based on your spot, so I will know who you are!"

I don't think anyone heard the last part. As AJ was speaking, a band as big as an army marched by to a military-style drum cadence. Their red-and-black uniforms, black hats and plumes gave them a menacing appearance, and every Hellcat watched as they passed. Their straight-backed drum major led their parade block with force and intensity. Awed, I couldn't pull my eyes away.

"That's the Marching Minutemen of Revolutionary

High," Steve whispered to me. "They always kick our butts in the parade category, but I think we have their number for field show this year." Their line seemed never-ending.

"They've been selected to march in this year's Darcy's department store Thanksgiving parade," Steve went on.

Okay, that was impressive. Like most people in America, I watched the parade on Thanksgiving morning while my parents got ready for the holiday. What an honor for this group!

I flashed back to the first day of band camp, when I thought all of this stuff was ridiculous. And, on some level, I knew that it kind of still was—especially to a real musician. But seeing the Minutemen sparked my competitive streak. So what if they were way bigger than us? Or louder? Or going to perform on national TV in a matter of weeks? We were going to kick their butt. I had a goal bigger than just playing my best—*winning*. I wanted that trophy! My heart pounded with excitement. I caught Jake's eye across the arc and gave him a smile. He grinned back, and I felt happy and light—like one of those parade balloons.

We formed our parade block—basically a rectangle, five people per row, and about a third smaller than the Minutemen—and AJ brought us to attention. I stood between Punk, who was in the center, and Steve, who marched on the outer left side.

AJ counted off and gave the forward march command.

My heart thudded over the drum line as I kept pace with Steve and Punk, careful to keep our line straight. We marched through the school parking lot to the inspection station, where we stood at parade rest while AJ waited for the judges' signal.

When he got it, he called us to attention in a loud, clear voice. We snapped into position.

One hundred twenty-five people held their breath.

Seconds later, a clipboard-carrying judge was in front of me. I smelled his grape bubble gum. Using all of my concentration, I kept my eyes locked straight ahead. Even when, surrounded by a cloud of synthetic grape-ness, the judge leaned in to examine something on my shoulder, I didn't so much as flicker my glance in his direction. My stomach and heart danced a hot tango. I tightened my grip on my horn and waited for him to finish.

That's when the itch started. Right at the tip of my nose; it was like a tap-dancing butterfly had landed there. It was completely maddening, and there was nothing I could do about it.

My eyes filled with tears. The sensation was absolutely torturous.

And, I realized with growing horror, it was turning into an urge to sneeze.

15

Let's say there's such a thing as "sneaking" a delicate sneeze during parade inspection—which is nearly impossible anyway—there'd be no mistaking the lion-like sound I make when it happens. I squeezed my eyes shut tight, then opened them, hoping that would kill the urge.

No dice.

I tried breathing faster, then slower, to take care of it.

How long did inspection *last*? My nose tingled like ants were marching around in there.

Horrified, I realized it was out of my control.

My head flew back, mouth opened, and I let loose—just as AJ's whistle gave us the signal to move forward.

The sneeze roared out of me even louder than I expected. A fine mist settled over my mellophone, which I still held at attention. My hat slipped, visor covering one eye. In my peripheral vision, Steve winced. The trumpet player in front of me cringed, and it may have been my imagination, but I swore that AJ's plumed hat became just a little bit straighter out of aggravation.

The drummers tick-tick-ticked a straight beat for us until we reached the parade's starting line. Then AJ put us in parade rest and gave us the at ease command. Before Steve could say anything, I fixed my hat and raised one hand in the "stop" gesture.

"I know. I know!" I said, near tears. "I did everything I could to stop it, but nothing worked."

"Actually," Steve said dryly, "I was thinking about changing your nickname from Chicken to The Bomber. How does such a big noise come out of such a small person?"

Ha-ha. Steve's lame attempt at humor only made me feel worse. AJ called us to attention. Time to step off.

Our marching cadence—what the drummers play between songs when we're on the parade route—started. More than just a simple tick-tick-tick to keep us marching in step, the cadence has a groove to it, like a percussion-only song, and its heavy bass beat triggered car alarms all along the residential street as we marched.

"Whoop-whoop!" called someone behind me in the parade block—probably a drummer. I grinned, post-sneeze guilt nearly gone.

Spectators lined the parade route. I kept in line with Punk and Steve, holding my head high. After twice through the cadence, AJ signaled us to start playing our medley of marches. We played through that twice, then it was back to the cadence. Repeat.

After three repetitions, the excitement wore off. I had no idea how long the route was—someone had mentioned three miles, but it felt as though we'd been walking for ten. Band parents and Mr. Sebastian wove through the parade block, offering us sips from water bottles when we weren't playing.

Finally I spotted the review stand ahead on my left. A small crowd sat on portable bleachers. The judges' table was down in front. We'd march through, and the judges would score us based on our sound and marching precision.

Before I had time to think, AJ counted off. Unlike never-ending inspection, what seemed like a second later I'd crossed the far side of the review area. We hadn't even finished playing the whole piece.

From there, it was about the length of a football field to the end of the parade. When we crossed the finish line and AJ put us at parade rest, a wave of exhaustion hit me.

"Good job, people!" AJ called to the whole group. He was standing near Steve, shouting so the entire band could hear him. Then, quieter, to us, "I want to know who the sneezer is. *Now*."

I lifted my head to confess.

"Me," said a voice from my right. Punk. Covering for me *again*! What was it with him?! Well, this time I wouldn't let Punk take my punishment—based on AJ's glare, running laps would be a treat compared to what he had planned. I opened my mouth to protest when a parade volunteer came up to AJ and whispered in his ear.

"Picture time!" he called to everyone. And, only to Punk, "We'll talk later."

We were still in parade block, so AJ marched us to the photographer while I wondered what was up with Punk. Portable bleachers had been installed in a local park, and the notorious Marching Minutemen stood on them, finishing their formal picture. Even post-parade, they seemed intense. Especially their drum major, whose eyes were downright scary.

"I heard he makes their whole band run laps before practice," Punk stage-whispered to me. "People yurked during their band camp."

I shuddered. The Minutemen were so intimidating, it wouldn't have surprised me.

"You don't have to keep covering for me," I whispered to him. He stared straight ahead at the Minutemen, like he hadn't heard me.

"One, two, three!" shouted the photographer. A flash. "Beautiful! Beautiful! Okay, now quick—set up a silly picture!"

In a blur of red and black, kids scrambled into funny poses—a group of trumpets raised a piccolo player above their heads, some trombones stuck their hats on the slides of their instruments, and the sousaphones coordinated some goofy gangsta signs.

Crack!

I jumped, the sound so loud that my inspection station sneeze seemed like a whisper.

Steve pointed to the other band.

The Minutemen in the middle of the bleachers seemed to be standing a step lower than the kids around them.

Then they disappeared.

16

Right after the collapse, it was total chaos for what felt like two hours, but was really only about ten minutes. AJ, Mr. Sebastian, and every available parent and volunteer rushed toward the Minutemen, shouting for cell phones and to call 911. We broke formation immediately and also rushed forward to help, but were scooted back by the adults. I huddled with Jake, Steve, Sarah, and Punk, unable to tear my eyes away from the scene. Kids were crying and yelling that they were trapped; some were walking around, calling their friends' names, hurt and bleeding. Punk just kept muttering *"Dude"* over and over again, under his breath.

My hands shook, and my mellophone—which I refused to put down, it felt like it was my anchor—wobbled and jiggled. Steve noticed and put his arm around me.

"That could've been us," I said. "We were next. That could've—"

"Shhhh," he soothed, and gave my shoulder a reassuring squeeze. "It wasn't. We're okay."

"But they're *not!*" I cried. I heard the hysteria in my voice. I clamped my jaw shut and concentrated on breathing.

AJ and Mr. Sebastian ordered most of us back to the bus, but asked the biggest guys—mostly seniors on drum line and the sousaphone players—to stay and remove the Marching Minutemen's gear. Later, we found out that they also held up sections of the broken bleachers so that the paramedics could get to the kids trapped underneath.

Back at the buses, I sat with Sarah, Hector, and Jake on a towel in the sun. Wailing sirens and heavy horns comprised the disaster soundtrack playing in the background. Each time an ambulance left—I counted thirteen of them—the noise would get louder as it raced through the parking lot near us, then would lessen and finally fade as it sped to the hospital. We didn't say anything until the last siren echoed into the distance. I checked my watch. It had taken nearly two and a half hours to get every kid out. Sarah's eyes were puffy and red from crying.

Jake let out a big breath, like he'd been holding it the entire time we'd been sitting there. "Hope everyone's okay," he croaked, voice rusty.

"Yeah," said Hector.

I bit the inside of my cheek and swiped my sweating

hands on the towel for the thousandth time. Having the sirens gone was a relief, but now it was *too* quiet.

"What happens next?" My own voice sounded gravelly and rough. No one had an answer.

"I mean, we can't just go on with the competition, can we?"

"We can." All of us turned to find a pale, exhausted-looking AJ. "Meeting behind bus two in ten minutes," he said, and moved on to the next group.

"What is this, a 'show must go on' moment?" I blurted. "Those kids got *hurt*." This would end their season. And, I thought sadly, they'd lose their Darcy's parade spot.

"And they were here to perform," Jake gently reminded me. "That's what we do. Some of the groups have traveled a long way to be here."

I didn't like what he was saying, and, apparently, neither did Sarah. She turned around and started sniffling, but didn't speak. Hector stood up and stretched, then he shook his head, shrugged, and just walked away.

A few minutes later we joined the whole ensemble. Everyone looked worn—pale, sad, and just wiped out. Especially Punk, without his facial piercings. Their absence made him look like a boy instead of a rocked-out upperclassman. Seeing him like that unnerved me almost as much as the accident. I put my mellophone down and wrapped my arms around my body.

"It's been a tough day," AJ started. "And that's an

understatement." He paused, trying to find the right words for the group. "I don't have magic words to make us feel better. That was pretty awful and scary. A lot of our guys stepped up to help the Minutemen out, and you made us proud." Mr. Sebastian stood to the side, letting AJ lead us.

"The field show competition hasn't been canceled. Several groups have traveled from out of state to be here, and the judges felt that it wouldn't be fair to close the whole competition. They are giving the bands the option as to whether or not to perform tonight. I think we should be out there. The Minutemen are from our part of the state, and they're tough competitors. They worked hard to prepare their show, and so did we. We can honor them by taking the field, putting on our best show, and respecting the work that we do.

"It'll be hard, and I know a lot of us are totally upset by what we saw today." Was he looking directly at me when he said that part? "So I understand if you don't feel up to it. We're going to vote. If the Screaming Hellcats are going to take the field, *you* need to want it—not because I want to or anyone else thinks we should. So, show of hands: Who wants to perform?"

For a second, no one moved. Not one hand went up. Then, from the drum line, a few hands crept to the sky.

"We've been prepping since August. The Minutemen would want us to bring it," someone said.

That did it. All around me, hands reached up. Mine was still firmly at my side. How could we do this? How could *I* do this? Just the thought of getting out there, behind my instrument, made my insides watery.

Behind my instrument. That was the one place that I'd always been able to express my emotions. And blowing my face off tonight, surrounded by the people I was starting to see as real friends, would make me feel better. Before I could think about my decision—or that I was mentally referring to the once-hateful mellophone as "my instrument"—my hand shot to the sky. AJ gave me a big smile.

"Sweet. We're on at eight thirty. Be in uniform by seven fifteen. Dismissed."

17

The next couple of hours flew by. Jake pulled a Frisbee out of his bag and pulled together a game of Ultimate. When he came over to me, expression hopeful, I shook my head.

"Too much work," I explained. It bummed me out to say no to him for the zillionth time, but what else could I do? I was swamped. Hector, Sarah, Steve, and the others all joined the game, of course, leaving me alone by the buses.

I managed to read some of *Emma* (why does that girl feel the need to mess with everyone else's love life?), answered a couple of history questions, and even jotted some halfhearted notes for bio. The one thing I *wanted* to do? Practice for Shining Birches. But my French horn was at home—and even if I did have it, my mouth was still buzzy-feeling from the morning's parade, and I had to save my chops for the field show competition.

A little before seven, just as the sky was starting to

turn pink, Sarah and I grabbed our uniform bags from the bus and got dressed again. She seemed much happier—maybe all that running around during Ultimate Frisbee helped her out?

The band assembled in front of the buses, and we lined up in parade formation again. We had to march from the parking lot to the outside of the community college stadium across the street. My parents would be in the stands. They'd skipped the morning's parade because my dad was subbing for a friend on *Wicked*'s matinee. I wondered if they knew about the collapse.

We marched over to just drum ticks, no cadence. Everyone's faces were set and solemn. There was none of the excitement or anxiety that came before the parade competition that morning. Instead, the overwhelming feeling was of determination. In spite of what happened, standing next to Steve and Punk made me feel strong.

The sun had almost totally gone down, and the lower half of the sky was a deep navy blue; above it was indigo. We stopped and did a low, slow warm-up, then got back in formation and waited to be introduced. Out of respect for the Minutemen, AJ didn't call out any of the Hellcats' pre-performance goofy chants or cheers, which only added to the strange, surreal feeling I had. It was like being part of a different group.

"From Auburnville, Massachusetts, we are proud to present the Screaming Hellcats of Henry Herbert High.

They will be performing their field show, music from *West Side Story*. Welcome, Hellcats!" Applause poured from the crowd.

We marched in during the introduction, and were now set in our positions to take the field. I took a second to glance around the stadium.

It was packed.

From my perspective, it looked like every seat was filled. Smaller bands who had already marched and were still dressed in uniform sat on one set of bleachers, but the rest of the stands were stuffed with spectators. Parents, kids, band staff, community members—there had to have been over a thousand people up there. This was, by far, the largest audience I'd ever played in front of.

My respectful mood disappeared, replaced by excitement and a thrill of fear. AJ counted off and we took our spots on the field. On his podium, his white uniform contrasting with our black ones, he looked military-sharp.

"One! Two! One-two-three!" he shouted, and we played.

The sound filled me like it had on the first day of band camp, its power taking me by surprise. I almost forgot to step off.

I marched across the field, playing my part, moving smoothly to my first spot. Out of the corner of my eye, I could see that my line was perfectly straight. We stepped off into the next set as a unit. The flags spun and floated past us, every girl in color guard making her spins and working in perfect unison. Sarah would be psyched. I stopped thinking, letting my body carry me through the show while I played my instrument.

During the final number, "Somewhere," we marched a company front, shoulder to shoulder. I felt locked in with the whole ensemble, pushing our wall of sound straight at the audience, trying to knock AJ off his podium with what came out of my bell. The hair on my arms stood straight up and I had chills.

Our last note resonated across the field.

The crowd roared over the ringing in my ears.

On the sidelines, we jumped up and down and hugged one another.

"Freakin' *awesome*!" Punk cheered.

"Whoo! High brass rules!" screamed Steve.

Shouts and whoops echoed through the band. AJ came over for high fives. "Incredible! You guys nearly took me out during that company front!" He laughed. "Elsie, I thought you were going to knock me over with what was coming out of your bell!"

I beamed.

We didn't have a ton of time for celebrating, though, as we had to watch the two bands scheduled to perform after us. The Minutemen were supposed to have gone on last, and when it was their turn, the announcers came on and

119

asked for a moment of silence and for our prayers to go out to those band members and their families. I wondered how the kids were doing, and if we'd find out.

Then all of the bands returned to the field. We stood in clumps according to our size and performance category while they gave out the awards.

For the parade competition, we hadn't placed in our category. The Marching Minutemen, however, had—they took first. The stadium erupted in huge cheers for them.

Then it was time for field show. I fidgeted as they worked their way through the two categories below us. They reached our group and I held my breath.

"Third place, with a score of eighty-nine point three, are the Dover Dolphins!" On our left, a band from New Hampshire started screaming. Their drum major stepped forward and saluted the judges before taking the trophy.

The judge returned to the podium.

"Second place, with a score of ninety point one, the Reading Rockets!" My breath wooshed out. Two down.

"And in first place, with a score of ninety point four," the judge began. I couldn't inhale again, just stood, not breathing, clutching Sarah's and Hector's hands, "the Screaming Hellcats of—" but I didn't hear any more. A scream bomb went off all around me. Hector pulled Sarah and me into a group hug.

We won! By three tenths of a point!!

I screamed too.

18

My parents found me back at the buses and congratulated me. My mom was weepy—the same way she gets every time I perform. Dad was his typical reserved self, but something seemed a little different about him. And honestly, I didn't really care what it was. I was too busy checking out our shiny new trophy, squirting Silly String and dodging Silly String squirted at me (someone had thoughtfully packed an Emergency Celebration Kit) to care.

Mom and Dad hovered around the band parents, who made sure that we'd properly packed our uniforms before the stringy celebration began. Then, as I was standing with Steve and Punk, reliving the show for the zillionth time, my dad approached.

"We really need to get going, Elsie," he said. "Mom and I will wait while you say your good-byes."

I was confused. "What do you mean, you'll wait?"

Steve gave me a quick hug and Punk slapped high

fives with me, then they edged away. Dad's face was red.

"Please get your things and we can walk over to the car together."

Huh?

Then I realized—my father thought I was going to ride home with him and Mom! Uh, no way.

"I'm taking the bus back," I explained.

"I'm going to speak with Mr. Sebastian about it now. Please go get your things," he repeated.

My post-victory glow dimmed like a disappearing ghost.

"But I *want* to take the bus," I said, trying to stay calm. Didn't he get it? There'd be celebrating, and cheering, and passing the trophy around. I wanted to be there for that. To be part of it.

"I'm sure you do. But you'll see your friends on Monday," he said in his clipped "this discussion is over" voice. I looked around for Mom, who gave me a sympathetic smile.

"Sweetheart, it's okay," she said. "There'll be other opportunities to celebrate."

"You can't be serious."

"Get your things," Dad ordered.

"But Steve would be—"

Dad cut me off.

"Get your things and let's go."

"Fine." I turned and stomped away, tears stinging my eyes. He was cutting my celebration short! Okay, we hadn't just played Wagner's Ring Cycle or gotten off the stage at the Met, but this was a big deal to me.

I slammed up the bus stairs, making as much noise as I could, and grabbed my bag, hatbox, and instrument. This was *so* not fair. Other kids' parents were letting them take the bus home. Why couldn't I? And why hadn't Mom and Dad thought to mention this game-changer before I left?

I stood on the blacktop outside of the bus, clutching my stuff, fuming and halfheartedly searching for my mom and dad. I spotted them over by Mr. Sebastian and the band parents, then took my time getting there. I didn't want to go around and say good-bye to everyone, making it totally obvious that I was leaving early.

As I approached, I heard my dad saying, "Since we drove out here for the competition, it only makes sense that she come home with us directly instead of us having to meet the bus at school. And we feel that it's just too much responsibility for a student driver, especially after dark. It's not safe."

I stood stock-still. *What?! What?!* They were taking me home because it was *too much trouble for them* for me to ride home on the bus? And too dangerous to be with Steve? That it was *unsafe*? What did they think was going to happen?

"Are you kidding me?" I snapped, startling the entire group.

"Oh, honey," my mom said, "don't be upset. It's not

like that." She must have seen the anger in my expression, because she stepped back. Mr. Sebastian and the band parents moved away to give my family fight some privacy.

"You are making me come home with you because it's too much trouble for you if I take the bus home? That it's dangerous for me to ride with Steve?! Are you *crazy*?" I yelled directly at my dad, in front of all those people, and the worst part was, I couldn't stop myself.

"Not crazy. I'm your father," he snapped back. "Just in case you've forgotten your relations as well as your manners, Elsie. Do not be disrespectful."

"You're being disrespectful to *me*!" I wailed. Today had been a crazy roller coaster of emotions and I was stretched as thin as a drumhead. Much to my chagrin, tears burst through and I started crying. I couldn't help it.

"See? You're tired. You need to go home. It's only a marching band competition," he said.

I gasped, heart in my mouth.

"Let's go," he said, as though he didn't see how hurt I was.

"I am not tired!" I said through my tears. "I'm just— just—"

Just fed up with how you treat me.

Just wishing you would see me as a player ready for Shining Birches.

Just wondering how I ever thought we were so alike.

Just wondering why I ever wanted to be like you.

But I couldn't bring myself to say any of that. I don't even think I had the right words.

"Honey, let's go." My mom's quiet voice cut through my fury like a hot knife through butter. All of my anger melted away, a puddle of disappointment left behind.

"Yeah, sure."

"We'll discuss your behavior at home, young lady," my father said with one last stern look. They turned and started walking to the car.

I just stood there for a few seconds, allowing them to put some distance between us. Why was Steve driving me home from school such a big deal? Why did Dad act like this ensemble, and its achievements, didn't matter or weren't worth celebrating? Sure, it was a marching band—not Shining Birches or the BSO—but we'd just put on a kickin' show!

Reluctantly, dragging my feet, I followed them through the parking lot maze. What if I didn't go with my parents? What if I veered off, ran around and ducked into one of the buses to hide . . . until Mom and Dad realized I was missing and started thinking I'd been kidnapped. Then they'd tear the whole competition area apart. That'd be not so awesome.

All of this was my father's fault. But, seriously, what had caused him to act all freaky and why hadn't my mom stood up for me? I was so preoccupied with my thoughts, I stopped paying attention to my parents. When I glanced up, I couldn't spot them at all. Maybe they'd reconsidered and left me behind? Although highly unlikely, the thought made me grin.

Then, from right in front of me, Dad's long frame appeared.

"Elsie! There you are! I thought we lost you!"

His comment snapped me back from my daydream-y moment, and I instantly filled with humiliation-stoked rage.

"Of course you didn't lose me," I snapped. "Where am I going to go? Hang out with my friends? Not like I'll have any after this."

His hands, extended to take my hatbox and mellophone case, clenched into fists and he stuffed them in his pockets. Fine. I would carry my own stuff, no problem. I saw him take a deep breath and let it out slowly as he turned.

I purposely kept slightly behind him as we walked.

Okay, I didn't walk. I stomped.

"I don't know what's gotten into you lately, young lady," he said through clenched teeth. We reached the car. Mom leaned against its side, waiting. She arched an eyebrow when she saw us, but she didn't say anything.

"What's gotten into *me*?" I cried as I tossed my mellophone case and hatbox into the trunk. "You just completely embarrassed me for no reason. *That's* what's gotten into me!"

I thumped into the backseat and pressed my body into the corner against the window.

"We didn't intend to embarrass you, honey," Mom said. "Your father and I thought that this would just be a simpler solution than having you ride the bus and then getting you at school."

"Oh come on!" Her mild tone just made me more frustrated. "No one else gets taken home by their parents. We celebrate on the bus! You also said it was too dangerous for me to ride home with Steve. I heard you!" I squeezed the edge of the seat.

"You can celebrate your achievement on Monday," Dad replied, sounding just as aggravating. "And, if I remember correctly, we had a conversation on the first day of school about rules, Elsie, and you have flagrantly violated them. Plus you were incredibly rude to me in front of those parents."

I leaned forward, between them. "Steve is my section leader—that's it!—and you know it. And I wouldn't have been rude if you hadn't said that stuff about me in the first place." How had this happened? It was supposed to be my night to shine, and instead I was fighting tears, dragged home like a naughty toddler.

"We're just watching out for you, Elsie," Mom said. "I understand that you're upset, but you have to put yourselves in our shoes too. It's been a long day for *everyone*." She gave my dad her "I disapprove of your behavior" face:

raised eyebrows and a frown. We rode the rest of the way in silence, my anger glowing like hot coals, and when we got home I marched into the kitchen and turned to my parents.

"Despite what you think, I am *not* a child! Stop treating me like a baby!" Unable to control my tears, I raced up to my room and slammed the door.

Real mature, huh?

19

I sulked over the competition for about a week. We'd be in the middle of recapping the show and the awards ceremony when Hector or Sarah or Jake would mention something about what happened on the bus after—how Punk had led the group in a hilarious song, or how AJ had given this great post-competition speech—and this stabbing pain would attack my heart. I'd get quiet or walk away.

At home, my parents decided that my "explosive, disrespectful behavior" the night of the competition earned me limited computer time and no phone calls for a week. Some punishment—I practiced so much I barely had time for either. But the whole situation made me even more angry with my dad. He didn't see value in marching band. He didn't think I could get in to Shining Birches. He didn't think I could handle anything. He didn't believe in me.

I'd show him. I'd knock his socks off.

I started practicing like a fiend; any time that I wasn't at school, doing homework, or rehearsing for marching band, my French horn was at my lips. My private teacher, Mr. Rinaldi, was impressed with my progress, but really harped on me to keep to a rigorous practice schedule. Since my dad kept odd hours, there were plenty of opportunities for practicing at home when he was also around—and I didn't want that. So I had to plan my time carefully. All that work felt good. Sure, I didn't have time to hang out with Jake or Steve or Hector and Sarah that much, but it was worth it. Or it would be. Sometimes being great means being lonely, I guess.

But spending so much time alone with my horn wasn't as easy as it had been last year. I still loved playing, loved how I felt when the music flowed from the bell, but I was also aware of what I was missing—Sarah's fashion babble, Hector's goofy movie score questions, and Jake's . . . well . . . *Jakeness.*

And, oh, yeah, then there was that little issue of telling my parents about the dance. With my "restrictions" still in place, I hadn't wanted to mention anything about it, just in case they decided that removing the one social opportunity I had all semester would be a better punishment.

But the date was getting too close to put off the conversation any more, and one night after dinner I went for it.

"So," I began, "HeHe High has an annual, uh, dance for Halloween. And I am planning to go with Sarah and . . . a few other band people," I finished lamely, realizing that announcing I'd be attending with Jake and Hector wouldn't win me any points. Let my parents figure that part out for themselves.

"When?" Mom asked. I told her the date, and she shook her head.

"Elsie, your father has a BSO performance that night. I was hoping we could all go as a family. We haven't been this season because your schedule has been so busy."

"We're playing Tchaik *V*," Dad added.

As much as I loved Tchaikovsky's Fifth Symphony, I had made a promise to my friends—who I hadn't seen in forever. And since the post-band competition blowup, I wanted nothing to do with my parents.

"I can't," I said.

"You need to communicate better, Elsie," my mom snapped, losing her patience with me. Her back was against the stove, I was seated at the table, Dad leaning in the doorway.

"Well, so do you," I retorted. "I'm in high school, remember? There's more to my life now than concerts and rehearsals!"

"We understand that," my dad said, trying a softer approach, "but *you* have to understand that there's more to this than scheduling. We won't be home to pick you up or drop you off. And we don't like you staying home alone."

Still fuming, I considered what he said. "I can get a ride with someone else's parents," I said, not sure if I could, but knowing it was the only way to go to the dance. "You can drop me off at Sarah's on the way and I can get ready there. Her mom will drive me. And the dance gets out after the concert, anyway, so you could pick me up on your way back."

Mom and Dad shot looks at each other, exchanging telepathic parental signals.

"I'd have to speak with Sarah's mother," Mom said.

That was the cue that I'd won.

I nodded, suppressing a smile. "Of course."

Dad scowled. "Along with missing Tchaikovsky, you'll miss the chance to meet Richard Dinglesby."

My heart tugged. Richard Dinglesby was the director of Shining Birches.

But what about the promise I made to my friends? I reminded myself. Our costume worked as a team, and I'd be letting them down if I went to the performance. Plus, the Shining Birches auditions were blind. Richard Dinglesby would have no idea whether or not we'd met when I was sitting behind a screen, playing my horn.

And, I realized, I kind of *wanted* to go to the dance. Like it was a reward for the extra-hard work I'd been putting in lately.

"Dad, this is important to me too," I said.

The look on his face said: "Really? A dance is important?"

My insides churned, but I wanted to stand my ground. I'd originally decided to go to the dance because it would upset my dad. I just hadn't realized how much that would upset me.

20

That Saturday, before my private lesson, Mom brought me to Sarah's house to work on our costumes. Before getting out of the car, she gave me a peck on the cheek. I was a little nervous about hanging out with Sarah outside of school, so I didn't open the door right away. Instead, I fiddled with the straps on my book bag.

"You'll be back to bring me to Mr. Rinaldi's?" I asked, searching for a reason to prolong the drop-off.

"Of course. As it is, I don't like leaving you at someone's house that we've never met."

I didn't know it was possible to feel both nervous and annoyed at the same time, but there you go. I was.

"Mom, seriously, I *did* go to junior high with her. If her family are ax murderers, I think we'd know." I tried to keep my voice light. "Just be here at three, okay? If I'm not out, the police can start searching for my body." Without waiting for her to respond, I opened the door and slipped from the car, nerves gone. I gave her a big cheesy smile and wave before turning to go up the steps. So annoying!

Of course, that's when the anxiety kicked back in. I'd never been to Sarah's house before, let alone hung out with boys—I'd strategically left their presence out when telling Mom that we'd be doing costume prep—and what if her parents *were* ax murderers?

Before I could worry about it too much, the front door opened. Sarah stood there, Hector peering over one shoulder, Jake—all floppy hair and warm smile—over the other.

"It's about time!" she said. "Hector's been pestering us with another music question."

The three of them moved aside to let me in.

"My dad was watching this war movie from the seventies, and there's a scene with helicopters—"

I cut him off. "And the background music goes ba-da-da daa-daa, ba-da-da daa-daa, ba-ba-da-da-da . . . right?"

Hector's eyes widened. "How'd you know?"

"It's Wagner. 'Ride of the Valkyries.' It's one of the best horn pieces ever written. The Pops played it."

"Someday he's going to stump you," Jake said.

"Not if the Pops has ever played it." I grinned at him.

Sarah's house was different from mine—it was about three times as big and looked brand-new. She led us into the kitchen, where a marble island was covered in snack options: soda, cookies, chips, and popcorn.

"Mom left this stuff out for us," she said, scooping a

bowl of popcorn up in her arms. "She's upstairs, painting a piece of furniture or something. She's on a decorating kick." The boys stuck bottles of soda in their pockets and grabbed a small mountain of cookies while I pretended that this was normal for me too.

Sarah's family room had big, soft, cream-colored couches and an oversized TV hanging from the wall. Art supplies were scattered across a large square coffee table, fluffy throw pillows scattered around it on the floor. Sarah sat on one.

"So we've got felt and cardboard and markers and stuff," she said, making room for the popcorn bowl and her drink. Jake and Hector pulled pillows to opposite sides of the table. I dropped my bag and sat down too.

"I printed out pictures of all of the characters," Hector said. He unfolded a few sheets of paper that I'd seen sticking out of his back pocket.

"Are we going to make actual heads, or just try and dress like them?" I asked.

"I don't think we *could* make actual heads," Jake said. "Plus, that might look too dorky for high school. How about we settle on one or two features per Muppet, and make those?" We all liked that idea.

"Janice wears a cool hat sometimes," Hector said, pointing to one of the photos.

"I could do that, and do my makeup like hers," Sarah said. Jake would make Kermit's green neck pattern (what do you call that thing?) and Hector needed a hat and tie for Fozzie.

"Miss Piggy wears a giant pearl necklace," Sarah said carefully, as though afraid I'd blow up. "And you could make ears too. We could put them on a headband."

"Okay," I answered. I was determined to be pro–Miss Piggy. "Sounds great!" My second big cheesy smile of the day.

We started working, chatting about classes and teachers and band. Things were going fine until Jake put down a piece of green felt and leaned over the table.

"So, Elsie, what's up with you practicing so much for Shining Birches? I mean, I love my trumpet and all, but you take music appreciation to the next level." His lopsided smile softened his words.

"Nothing's up." I shrugged and fiddled with a pipe cleaner, rolling it into the shape of a horn. "I just want to get in, so I have to practice a lot."

"That's an understatement." Sarah rolled her eyes. "You don't do anything else *except* practice."

Jake shot her a look, but continued to push me.

"I mean, you're a superstar musician, but most people don't apply until junior year. What's the big deal about getting in?"

Anger knotted my insides and I crumpled the pipe cleaner sculpture. They don't get it, I reminded myself. It's not their life. I needed to explain it nicely.

"There is no deal. It's just . . . I really want to go *now*. Music is what I want to do for the rest of my life, and I just don't want to miss an opportunity." There. That should satisfy them. I straightened the pipe cleaner and smoothed it against the leg of my pants.

"Yeah, I get that," Hector said, "but you're kind of killing yourself over it. Like you'd lose something if you don't get in."

His words stung. The same frustrated, hopeless feeling I had at the band competition came back and mixed with anger. And before I could get it under control, my mouth opened.

"I want to beat my dad." The words were a shock, even to me.

"Beat your dad at what?" Sarah perched her Janice-hat on her head.

"He went there when he was a junior," I explained, feeling my face redden, "and I want to beat that, and get in as a freshman. It'd be the one musical . . ." I searched for the right word, "*achievement* that would be mine first. It's kind of important to me." It was weird—I'd been practicing for and thinking about Shining Birches forever, but it had never occurred to me that part of the reason why I wanted it so badly was to show up my dad. At least, I didn't *think* it had been about showing him up until I overheard him saying he thought I couldn't get accepted.

"Why?" Jake's hazel eyes pinned me to the truth.

"Because he doesn't think I can handle it, or that I'm good enough. But music is all I've ever been good at. Playing makes me feel like *me*." I blurted the words like I was spitting out a mouthful of rotten fruit. A few tears trickled down my cheeks, and I wiped them away. How embarrassing. "Sarah, where's the bathroom?"

She pointed and I fled into a potpourri oasis. I stood at the sink, dabbing my eyes and trying to get myself under control. I didn't want anyone thinking I was a freak, but I couldn't help my emotional explosion. High school was such a mess. It seemed that everything I did or said was wrong, and who I thought I was changed every day. The one thing that didn't change: what I wanted to be. A player who got in to Shining Birches. When I felt better, I went back to the group.

"Sorry," I muttered.

"No biggie," Jake said.

Hector nodded.

"We get it," he said. "My parents are always pushing me to do stuff, wanting me to be better, so I guess I have the opposite problem. They can't understand why I'm not as good at math and science as my sister. I remind them that not every Chinese kid is good at algebra. It doesn't help."

"My brother graduated from HeHe last year," Jake said quietly. "He was drum major, ran track, and was in all honors classes. My parents are pretty cool with not pressuring me, but it's like I'm walking around in his shadow when we're at school. I like music more than sports and want to do jazz band in the spring, but the track coach keeps bugging me."

Sarah piped up, "And if you hadn't noticed, my house is, like, a museum. If I make the slightest bit of a mess and don't pick it up immediately, my mom gets crazy. Like, she'll go a little nutty after you leave, and I'll be vacuuming and dusting forever." She tossed her hair and smiled. "So I leave my bedroom like a pigsty to drive her nuts."

I giggled.

"I'm glad it's not just me," I said. "I was starting to think stuff was so hard because I'm younger than everyone in our class."

Jake laughed, but in a nice way. "Oh yeah, Elsie. That's it—you're having a hard time because of your age."

"Seriously, though," Sarah added, eyes level with mine, "having fun sometimes is okay, Elsie. Even though you want to *be* a professional French horn player, you don't have to act like one all the time." Hector and Jake nodded in agreement.

Sarah's words felt like arrows piercing right to the center of my life. I *hadn't* been having fun this year . . . unless I was with this group. Before that, I couldn't remember having fun since Alisha moved . . . until the band competition. Sharing the family weirdness with them made me feel a little better too, but I couldn't help but think that there was something about my situation that was more intense than theirs—or maybe it was just me who was more intense?

Sarah showed me how to make two sets of Miss Piggy ears to sew together and line them with pipe cleaners so they'd stand up. Then we made a giant pearl necklace. I stuck with my new, positive, "I love Miss Piggy" attitude and nobody brought up Shining Birches. Actually, I started to have fun. I laughed when Hector did his C3PO impression and when Jake told us how he and his brother accidentally got locked in their uncle's car. I even told them about how I got stuck getting out of an awful peach dress that I was trying on for my cousin's wedding last spring. The zipper was broken, and I got it halfway over my head before I realized that it wasn't going to fit over my shoulders. Mom and the department store lady came running and cut me out with scissors.

Everyone cracked up. When I glanced at the clock, I saw it was time for me to leave.

"The dance is going to be really fun, Elsie," Jake said as he handed me my ears. "We'll be great together."

Our hands brushed as I took my costume pieces from him, and an electric shot zinged up my arm. I nearly dropped my book bag.

"Yeah," I grunted, sounding like a pig and mortified at the way the word fell from my mouth. Where did that jolt come from?

Okay, I knew where it came from. Jake and his . . .

Jakeness. My face burned. My palms started sweating. I couldn't look at Jake, just stuffed the costume deep into my bag while my heart slammed in my chest.

Sarah gave me a "what was that?" look, as though my arm was smoking from his touch. Which, it kind of was.

"Uh, well, thanks," I mumbled, squeezing past her and Hector on my way to the door and staying as far away from Jake as possible. "I'll see you guys on Monday." The last part was barely audible.

I threw the front door open and scuttled toward my mother's waiting car without a backward glance, arm humming.

That afternoon, I could barely focus on my lesson. My arm still felt tingly and warm, and twice Mr. Rinaldi had to stop me for silly mistakes.

"Earth to Elsie!" he joked, nudging me with an elbow.

I gave him a weak smile and settled my horn in my lap. "I'm here," I said. "Just a lot in my head today."

"Well," he said with a smile, "let's try and sweep those things out, then, and make way for some Brahms. The audition panel likes empty heads and full sound." He tapped his foot to set the pace of the piece, but I could barely hear it over my heartbeat.

21

By Friday night I was a jangle of nerves. My dad spent the afternoon skulking around with a hurt look on his face, and I was torn up over the decision I'd made. What if I was wrecking my chances at Shining Birches by going to the dance? I kept reminding myself that the audition was blind, that having fun was okay, and all of this was my choice, but it didn't help much.

Luckily, Sarah's mom had agreed to drive us to and from the dance—with a strict promise from Sarah to clean her room in return—and my mother seemed satisfied that Sarah's parents weren't ax murderers after all.

Mom wore a pretty blue dress, her blond hair piled on her head . . . and before we left, followed me around asking over and over again if I was sure I was comfortable going with Sarah. Dad, dressed in his BSO concert tuxedo, took the opposite approach—he gave me a peck on the cheek and told me to have fun, but his white-knuckled hands on the steering wheel said something else entirely. By the time my parents' car pulled up to Sarah's, I was relieved to escape.

"Enjoy yourself, sweetie," Mom said.

"Thanks," I mumbled, shifting my costume-filled backpack on my shoulder.

"Sure you don't want to change your mind?" Dad asked. I think he was trying to make a joke, but it didn't come across that way. Instead, it increased my guilt load.

This is my choice, I reminded myself for the thousandth time as I backed toward the house. My friends want me to be there with them. And, remembering that Jake-jolt, I wanted to be there. I waved at the car and turned to climb the front steps.

Sarah was at the door before I raised my hand to ring the bell. Excitement shot from her like lightning bolts. She grabbed my hand and dragged me to her room, the whole time chattering about how awesome we'd look in costume.

By the time she finished blowing out my hair and helping me apply layers of black gobby mascara and pink eye shadow, I was excited too. I wore a black dress from the zillions of concerts I'd played in, but Sarah contributed a hot-pink feather boa to my ensemble. Add my ears and faux-pearl necklace, and voila! Instant Miss Piggy!

"You look pretty good," she said, turning me to check out my reflection.

I smiled. "Not too bad," I said. I'd drawn the line at wearing a pig snout, though, so I hoped people got who I was.

"You look just like Janice," I said, happy to repay the compliment. Sarah's long hair—flat ironed to within an inch of its life—homemade hat, big eyelashes, heart-shaped mouth, and hippie outfit, made her a dead ringer for the Muppet.

"This is going to be awesome!" she said, grabbing my hand and leading me in a jerky twirl. "I am so psyched to see Hector and Jake." She danced around her room.

I smiled too, and squashed the nervous jig that started in my stomach at her mention of Jake's name.

Sarah's mom called out for us to hurry up or she'd leave us. We grabbed our stuff and headed downstairs.

"You two make a great pair," she said, barely glancing at us. She was scrubbing at a spot on the kitchen counter-top. "Coffee ring," she muttered.

On the ride to HeHe High, I wondered what Sarah would think of our house. I mean, we weren't slobs, but our house wasn't anywhere near as spotless as hers. My mom hated to vacuum, so my dad took over that chore. Frequently, he forgot to do it during the day, so the vacuum ran in the middle of the night, when he was back from a concert and needed to wind down. I'd long since learned to sleep through it—I even find it soothing, like white noise or whatever.

My mom dusted and did most of the laundry. I did my own clothes and sheets and stuff, but sometimes it'd pile up and my mom would do it for me. Mom wanted us to pick up, but magazines, random sheet music, homework papers, and financial documents littered the coffee table, dining room table, and various end tables. Shoes, like exhausted party guests, tumbled around every door.

The car pulled into the high school parking lot.

"You girls have fun and be safe," Mrs. Tracer said. "I'll be here at ten thirty to get you. Same spot. Sarah, do you have your cell?"

Sarah fumbled through her purse and waved it at her mother. Satisfied, Mrs. Tracer released the locks on our doors and we hopped out. We called out thank-yous as she pulled away.

"Ready?" Sarah asked. She tilted her Janice hat. I nodded, the rush of nerves filling my stomach again. Jake and Hector were supposed to meet us at the door of the gym, so we headed in that direction. As we crossed the quad, we caught sight of the juniors and seniors coming in from the parking lot. At least, I thought they were juniors and seniors. Most of the girls were wearing super-short skirts and glittery tops, and had their hair teased into huge poufs. A few were carrying white fluffy things, but I couldn't figure out what they were. One girl, a junior who was on color guard, passed us wearing what I swore was a sparkly headband as a dress. I couldn't control myself, I stopped and stared.

"They're bunnies." Jake's voice came from my left, zinging through me.

"Bunnies?" Sarah asked, confused.

"Yeah. The junior girls are all going as bunnies, and the guys are all going as . . . well, look." As Jake was finishing, a gaggle of guys wearing silky bathrobes and pajama pants came around a corner.

"Oh!" Sarah said. "Wow."

I was also wowed, and even though I still didn't get the exact point of the costumes, I knew they were risking dress code demerits in wearing them. And I also suddenly realized that our cutesy Muppets ensemble was *way* too cutesy for this dance.

I turned to tell Jake and Hector just that, and got a good look at the two of them. Hector had the tiny Fozzie Bear hat perched on top of his head, fuzzy ears sticking out from under it. A dark brown T-shirt made the white tie with red polka dots draped around his neck stand out.

"Wokka-wokka-wokka!" he said, and grinned.

Jake had found a vintage Muppets T-shirt, under which he wore a long-sleeved green tee. His Kermit the Frog felt collar lay around his neck like a punk necklace, and he'd gelled his hair into a spiky mess. Jake looked good. Very good.

"Wow," I said. "You don't look lame at all."

The boys smiled at each other. "Neither do you, Miss Piggy," Jake said, his voice low. My heart fluttered. He offered me his arm, and Hector stuck his out for Sarah. The four of us walked into the gym.

22

We'd been at the dance for an hour, but I hadn't danced at all—instead I'd spent most of the time playing name that tune with Hector and reminding myself to relax and have fun. Our group hung out in the corner of the gym with some of the other band kids—Steve was there, dressed as a mad scientist, and AJ came in wearing a light blue frilly tuxedo that was his dad's from the 1970s. Only he was cool enough to pull off bell bottoms. Even Punk made an appearance dressed as Frankenstein's monster, all of his piercings replaced with creepy bolts and screws and his hair dyed green for the occasion.

A few times, Sarah, Jake, and Hector had gone out on the dance floor, but I was just too shy. In public, I'd much rather play music than dance to it. Standing around gave me plenty of time to check out the other costumes, though. There were lots of *Dusk* vampires, of course, and the juniors had their skimpy-bunny thing going on (more than one of them were pulled aside by the chaperones). A few other groups had coordinated too: two Scooby gangs (glad we rejected that one), a James Bond with villains and Bond girls, and a group of seniors went as SpongeBob characters—complete with pineapple house.

The sophomore class was sponsoring the dance, and they'd decorated the gym with black and red streamers, fake spiders, and cottony cobwebs. It looked okay, but getting rid of the fried food smell would have really improved the atmosphere. I leaned against the wall, watching Hector and Jake bob and weave to a Styrofoam Rockets song with Sarah and a girl from the woodwind section.

"Dancing?" Punk appeared at my elbow. Up close I noticed that his face was painted light green.

"Not at the moment. Nice makeup," I responded, trying to change the subject. My stomach rolled into a ball. Would he ask me to dance? What would I say? It'd be so weird!

Punk cocked his head at me and then said something I couldn't hear over the pounding beat of the DJ's latest selection.

Heart slamming, I shook my head and made the international gesture for "I can't hear you": a quick shrug, second head shake, and pointing at an ear.

He leaned so close I could count the threads of the screw protruding from his nose. "I said, want to cut a rug, Chicken?"

My stomach dropped, feet tingled, and I felt perilously close to the way I had on the first day of band camp, just before I hit the ground. Punk wanted to dance with me? *With me?* I didn't know whether to be flattered or freaked out. I didn't like him, like him; I certainly didn't like dancing; and I didn't want to dance with him in front of anyone else—let alone *everyone* else. Especially, I had to admit, Jake.

Punk took my indecision for agreement. Grabbing my slick, sweaty hand, he led me onto the dance floor near the other band kids. Identical flashes of shock swept over their faces. I directed my eyes to my shoes. The music was fast and loud, and I briefly considered leaving Punk alone to enjoy it. But he'd probably come after me and do something even more humiliating. He danced with herky-jerky moves, arms flailing and elbows sticking out. Between his spastic movements and costume, he looked like an animated Tin Man . . . or a zombified one.

Not that I was much better. Still shocked and hit by waves of embarrassment, I stood, feet firmly planted on the floor, and attempted to dance by only shaking my shoulders from side to side. My hands and arms floated somewhere around my middle. The picture of grace. NOT.

Punk reined in his gyrations so he could get closer to me.

"You need to chill out, you know," he said over the music and into my ear. I tried to grin, but my cheeks were as tight as a snare drum head. I ended up baring my teeth.

"Seriously, Chick-chick," he went on, "have some fun. No one is dying around here. It's a *dance*. Enjoy it." He returned to his own dance space, then made a wild, arm-flapping, head-shaking turn combo—Frankenstein with rhythm. Other kids, band kids and non-bandees alike, stopped to watch him. When he noticed his audience he hammed it up even more: pigeon-bobbing his head, doing some seventies-inspired pointing, and shaking his hips like Elvis. The crowd—which I had backed into to escape Punk's spotlight—loved it.

And then he locked eyes with me and mimicked holding a fishing pole.

Everyone turned to me as he cast the line. Terrified, as though it were a real line with hook on the end, I followed its imaginary trajectory through the air, up, up, up and down, down, down, right to me.

Split-second decision time: Play it up or flee. My heart and stomach said to run away as fast as I could, but my legs were cemented to the floor.

The invisible fishhook landed. The crowd watched.

"It's okay to have fun," I whispered to myself. I took a deep breath, stuck my hands against my sides, tilted my chin to the ceiling, and hopped out of my spot toward Punk like a snagged tuna.

Punk mimed reeling me in, and I hopped closer, heart slamming, waiting for the fun to kick in . . . because now all I felt was nervous.

Everyone stared at me, wondering what was going on between us. I wondered the same thing. I didn't like Punk—I knew that—but I didn't know *what* his intentions were. Was all this because he like-liked me? Or was it just some weird joke?

I kept hopping a little closer each time, and he kept reeling. A few times I pretended to struggle against the line, and that got a laugh from those who were still watching. Thankfully, some kids had gone back to dancing and the song was nearly over. The whole thing reminded me of clucking like a chicken at band camp. Although this time, even though I was terrified, I forced myself to do it. And finally, once I got into it, it *was* kind of fun.

Just as the tune crashed to its end, I reached Punk. He squeezed my shoulders.

"Gotcha!" he said with a grin, and strode back to the side of the gym where we'd stood earlier. Breathless, I straightened my pig ears and followed.

As he leaned against the wall, the adrenaline left me, and annoyance—left over from being put on the spot—took its place.

"What was up with that?" I snapped, unable to control my tone of voice. Another upbeat dance tune slammed from the speakers.

"Jeez, Chicken," he said. He held his hands up in a mock "I surrender" pose. "Shoot me for wanting to have fun at a dance. Or wanting *you* to have fun for a change." I was tired of everyone (including myself) around me worrying about whether or not I was having fun—it made me feel even more awkward and lame.

"Why do you care whether or not I have fun? It's not your business," I said.

He stuck his hands deep in his pants pockets and pulled back. "You're right; it's not. It's not my business to try and save your butt in band either, but I've done that too."

Out of the corner of my eye, I saw Jake, Sarah, and Hector hovering nearby.

"I never asked you to do anything for me!" I cried, directing all my frustration at him.

"Don't worry. You won't catch me doing anything for you *ever again*." Punk pushed through the dancers, heading toward the door.

Before I turned to face my friends, I tried to compose myself. I was shaking. I'd just had a public fight with someone I barely knew over something I didn't understand, while wearing pig ears. Awesome.

"Uhh, Elsie?" Sarah stood at my elbow. "What was that about?"

I shook my head and mumbled, "I don't know."

She tugged my arm gently. "Let's take a walk, okay?"

I didn't resist, just let her guide me through the crowd, out of the caf, to the first-floor girls' bathroom. A gaggle of sparkly vampires huddled around the mirror, applying lip gloss and dishing about their dates. When they left, Sarah faced me.

"Spill it."

"There's nothing to spill," I said, tugging at my Miss Piggy necklace. "I don't know what happened." I summarized the events after we danced.

Sarah sighed. "Elsie, you bit his head off after he danced with you. *That's* what happened. Of course he's ticked." She paused. "Do you like him?"

The bathroom door opened, giving me a chance to think. Sarah was right—Elsie the Jerk strikes again. Tinker Bell flitted in, all fairy wings and pixie dust. Feeling deflated and helpless, I stayed silent until she disappeared into a stall.

"No!" I met Sarah's eyes when I said it. "Not at all. He's nice, and been really nice to me, but I don't like him, like him." Was that the third time I'd made that assertion in less than thirty minutes? Probably. "And, yeah, I acted like a total jerk back there." I blew out a puff of air. "Awesome."

"Pretty much," Sarah responded. "This is why people stay away from you, Elsie. You need to think about other people's feelings more." The words, unexpected and upsetting, made me gasp. She stopped, and I could see that she was upset too. Was I really that clueless about everyone else around me? As much as I didn't want to believe her, Sarah had no reason to lie to me.

When she went on, it was with a softer tone. "Whatever this deal is, you'd better figure it out, because someone's been waiting all night to ask you to dance, but got a no-dance vibe from you until that little scene. And it's not Hector."

Jake.

The hurt evaporated and my heart fluttered like Tinker Bell's fairy wings. She'd emerged from the stall and was washing her hands, a length of toilet paper stuck to one iridescent green shoe.

"Umm, 'scuse me?" I pointed at the damp strand.

She thanked me and scraped it off. Her voice was high and clear, the way an actual fairy's might sound. "I think you could use some fairy magic, Miss Piggy!" She pulled a silver wand from the bun in her hair and waved it around her head. "Ickle-sickle, gobble gubble! High school boys are nuthin' but trouble! Ickle-sickle, gobble gee! Pick the one that's right for *she*!" She bopped me on the nose with the wand and flitted out the door.

When it closed behind her, Sarah and I burst out laughing.

"The one that's right for *she*?!" I gasped.

"Ickle-sickle, gobble gow! Let us leave this bathroom *now*!" Sarah said through giggles.

On our way back into the gym, I realized I hadn't said anything to Sarah about Jake. I wanted to dance with him, but would he still want to dance with me after the scene with Punk? My hands started sweating at the thought, and a lump appeared in my throat.

We found Hector and Jake in basically the same spot where we'd left them, talking to AJ and Steve. Steve cocked an eyebrow at me and I frowned at him.

"Don't ask," I said.

"Oh What a Night," a song from the seventies that my mom dances to around the house, came on.

"Love this one!" AJ said. "Let's go find some of the color guard to dance with!" He tugged Steve's arm.

"As if they would," Sarah teased.

"Don't doubt my powers of persuasion, freshman," Steve growled, playful.

AJ grinned at the two of them. "Listen to your drum major! Dance!"

Hector and Sarah followed them into the crowd, leaving Jake and me alone.

"Hey," he said.

"Hey."

"Do you know this song?" he asked.

"My mom likes it," I said, suddenly shy. I wanted him to take my hand so I could feel that zing of electricity again, but I was also afraid that he would—or that its sopping wetness would gross him out.

Jake chewed his lip. "Want to dance?" He pointed to

the dance floor, where AJ was rocking out with two girls from color guard. "We could stay away from him."

I smiled. "Sure."

He held his hand out and I grabbed it. That shock shot through my arm, up my shoulder, and exploded my smile into a wide grin. We wove through the crowd to find Hector and Sarah, Jake not letting my hand go the entire time—in spite of its clamminess.

When we reached them, Sarah's eyes widened. Jake dropped my hand and faced me. I took the opportunity to casually wipe it on the side of my dress, hopefully drying it off. Jake bobbed his head and rocked his shoulders from side to side, like he'd been dancing his whole life. I shuffled across from him, aware of every dip and sway my body made, feeling wooden and awkward. Why did everyone else look more comfortable than me? Being younger than everyone else suddenly seemed to be a very big deal.

As much as my mom may like this song, it was not good for dancing.

It finally ended. I wasn't sure if I should cross the gym again—what if Jake wanted to keep going?—so I just kind of stood there. He did too.

The DJ's voice came from the speakers. "This next one is for couples only. It's a fan favorite by Theo Christmas, 'Her Majesty Cry.'" Soft strumming guitar filled the room. Around us, kids paired off and got close. Fear pinned me in place.

Jake stepped closer.

"Do you like this song?" he asked. His Kermit the Frog collar brought out green flecks in his eyes. He smelled soapy and faintly of Funyuns.

I nodded, unable to speak.

Jake took my right hand in his left, and brought it close to his shoulder. He slipped his other hand around my waist. I rested my profusely sweating palm on his shoulder, trying not to put any pressure on it in case the sweat soaked through his T-shirt. Our feet stumbled as I tried to figure out how this worked.

"Sorry," I said, stepping on his shoe. I was mortified. My hands were producing a catastrophic flood of fluid, my back was starting to sweat, and the smell of Funyuns became overpowering. Breathe, I reminded myself. Just breathe.

"Let me lead," he whispered.

"I'm not sure how!" I whispered back, face flaming.

"Just relax. Listen to the song."

I did what he said, focusing on the lyrics. "Couldn't smell your perfume in the air/Didn't see the flowers in your hair/Didn't know to trust that you were even there." I'd heard the song a million times before—it was on the radio every ten minutes, how could you not?—but hadn't realized how sad it was.

And while I was contemplating Theo Christmas's lyrical choices and emotional state, somehow, magically, I found myself slow dancing with a boy. Jake led us in a lazy circle of our little area of the dance floor. Unlike some of the other mashed-together couples, a foot of space was still between us, but we were slow dancing. I was *slow dancing*. With a *boy*!

And before I could stop myself, I realized how crazy that would make my dad. I stifled a grin at the thought of what he would say if he knew . . .

And forced my thoughts back to the present. This wasn't about what my dad would think or do—this moment was *mine*.

Jake's right hand rested on my back, hot as a stove burner. His left, clutching my right, I couldn't feel at all. I had it in a death grip and mine had gone numb. I loosened my fingers.

"Thanks," Jake said. "I was afraid I'd have to get it amputated at the end of the song."

"Sorry!" I whispered. "I had no idea."

"You don't have an idea about a lot of things," he said. My stomach felt like Jell-O. "Such as . . . ?" I said.

"Such as someone sitting a few chairs down from you at All-State might be impressed by your playing and your smile."

"Really?" I squeaked. I was in danger of fainting again.

"Or how cute your pig ears and annoying personality are."

"Oh." Breathe, Elsie, breathe, I admonished myself.

Luckily, Jake seemed to be done with torturing me with compliments and revelations. My head was spinning and I kept reminding myself to breathe. I didn't know what else to think, other than that I really, really liked him.

Jake steered us closer to Hector and Sarah, who were doing a dramatic, tragic imitation of a couple dressed as *Dusk* vampires that were clearly very serious about their love. We bumped into them and all of us laughed.

"Nice!" Jake said after Sarah dipped Hector. We broke apart to applaud them, and then Jake took my hand again. It was so easy . . . like he'd been holding my hand forever. I just wished I'd had a squeegee to mop it up before he grabbed it.

The song wound down, and Jake pulled me close.

"Elsie-Chicken," he whispered in my ear. The back of my neck prickled. "You are a fabulous Miss Piggy."

"And you are a fine frog," I said, trying to sound cooler and calmer than I felt—which was awkward and jangly and nervous-y.

The song ended, and Jake squeezed my hand. I smiled, firecrackers exploding in my chest. Was this real? Would it change things?

These questions and more bounced around my head to an andante beat. Jake led us off the dance floor and back to our corner of the caf. My smile was sandblasted on.

That is, until I spotted Punk watching us from the far side of the room.

23

I didn't know what to do. Should I go over to him? Apologize? Pretend like I didn't see him?

From where I was standing, it was hard to see the expression on his face, and I didn't want Jake to see him either. Even though nothing happened, I knew that would be a bad idea. I had no idea if Punk was angry or what. My giggly, whirly mood disappeared in an instant. My sweaty palms, not so much. Maybe the best thing would be to get Sarah and let her figure the whole thing out.

But when Jake and I got back to Sarah and Hector, Steve and AJ came over to us, a few color guard girls in tow, deciding that they needed to make a spectacle of whatever had happened—or not happened—as we danced.

"Tell us, Mr. Hopper. How does it feel to dance with a back-from-the-dead zombie chicken?" AJ waved an imaginary microphone in his face as Steve pretended to snap paparazzi photos. Jake's hand still firmly grasped mine, even though I tried to pull away.

"Let me tell you," Jake said, staring straight at me while speaking into the "microphone," "it was *clucking awesome!*"

Everyone—including me—busted out laughing. The laughter gave me an excuse to take my hand back. It wasn't that I wanted to let go of Jake, but I needed to collect my thoughts, my appendages, and dry my sopping palms. Again.

I moved a step or two away from his side and smiled when he glanced at me. I wanted him to know that I wasn't mad or anything, but I seriously needed to get some control back.

A few minutes later, the DJ played the last song. Jake was refereeing a heated discussion between Hector and one of the guys who played sousaphone over which family-friendly *Star Wars* aliens were more lame: Ewoks or Jar Jar Binks. Although he shot me an apologetic glance, I was grateful not to have to dance with him—or anyone—again. Too stressful.

When the lights came up, the four of us filed to the doors with the crowd. Headlights brightened the turnaround at the front of the school as parents lined up to collect those of us unable to drive.

"So," Jake said. And as soon as he said it, my palms started weeping.

"Yeah," I said, willing my hands to dry. Jake gave me

this cute half smile and my insides coiled tighter than the tubing of my horn.

"This was . . . nice."

Now I was a blushing and sweating Miss Piggy. Awesome. I probably smelled like a pig too, come to think of it. And that made me sweat and blush even more.

"Yeah." I couldn't think of anything else to say.

"My mom's here," called Sarah from a few feet away.

"Her mom's here." Somehow, Jake had gotten closer to me while we were talking. His arm brushed mine, searching for my hand.

Suddenly, the night was too much: Punk, the dance with Jake, everyone seeing us together, the general weirdness of the situation—it became overwhelming. I needed some time to think.

"Okay!" I called, louder than I needed to. "See you on Monday," I said with extra cheer in my voice. Jake's stunned expression stabbed me in the heart.

"Yeah," he mumbled, stepping back.

I brushed past him and raced to Mrs. Tracer's car. Sarah was already in the front seat. I hopped in back, heart pounding. As we drove away from HeHe High, I couldn't help but feel relieved that the night was over. When not behind my horn, I'd probably spend the rest of the weekend reliving and analyzing every moment of it.

Unfortunately, my parents had other ideas. I'd forgotten that we had dinner plans on Saturday night—friends of my mom invited us over. I didn't see why I had to go. The Abates' kids were in college and there'd be no one there for me to talk to. But Mom insisted that Mr. and Mrs. Abate wanted to "see how much I'd grown."

Dad had gotten a sub for his BSO gig; not that it mattered. He was late getting home from his practice studio, which made *us* late leaving, which made Mom really, really annoyed.

"Tell me why you are early for every single gig you play, but you can't seem to be *remotely* punctual for anything else," she groused from the front seat. Dad was driving like a maniac, as if he could break the space-time continuum and get us there before we were supposed to have left or something.

"I just got involved in the music." He glanced at me in the rearview mirror. "You know what that's like, right, hon? When you are so into what you're playing that everything else disappears?"

I totally did. But he wanted backup, I wanted to be anywhere else.

"Not exactly," I said, scowling. Mom gave a victorious "*Hah!*"

I stared out the window to avoid the hurt in his eyes.

When Monday rolled around, I didn't feel better about anything. As a matter of fact, I'd spent the remainder of the weekend so worried about what would happen when I saw Jake that I barely ate or slept, and felt awful. I even avoided the computer, in case he IM'ed me. My mom, convinced I was coming down with something, force-fed me some awful tea that my great-grandmother swore cured colds.

"Mom, seriously, I don't think I need this stuff," I croaked after a sip that made me gag.

"Finish the cup," she admonished. "You'll thank me later."

It tasted like black licorice and old shoes, but I choked it down under her watchful eye.

"Elsie," she said, once the cup was emptied to her satisfaction—no standing liquid, just a few dribbles at the bottom, "your father and I are concerned about you."

Inside, I groaned. Just what I needed, Mom and Dad on my case. I was stressed out enough. It was times like these I wish I had a younger sister or brother to distract them.

"I'm just busy," I replied, staring into the teacup. "That's all. There's nothing to worry about."

"Well, we want to make sure that you're still making good choices and taking care of yourself. You are under a great deal of pressure and we've noticed a change in your behavior."

Hmmm . . . like freaking out when you and Dad dragged

me away from my friends at the band competition, instead of going quietly? That's what I wanted to say. Instead, I just sat there, trying to look innocent and fighting the building aggravation.

Also, if I remembered correctly, "making good choices" and "taking care of myself" were parental code phrases for not doing drugs—illegal or otherwise. My mom goes on streaks where she watches every one of those newsy TV shows—you know, the ones where they devote an hour to profiling some girl who stole her friends' ADHD medicine at a slumber party, then raced into the street while hopped up and got hit by a truck—and then she gets all uber-parental on me. If this weren't my life, it'd be really funny.

Mom went on, "We're also concerned that marching band might be taking up too much of your schedule. You're doing schoolwork and practicing at odd hours." She folded her hands on top of each other.

Whoa—was Mom suggesting that I needed to quit marching band? What would happen to my chances at Shining Birches if I did *that*?!

"I am making excellent choices, Mom," I replied, struggling to keep my voice even, "*and* finishing my homework, doing fine in all of my classes, and still able to practice my horn. Seriously; I'm okay." As I spoke, I gathered my lunch and books, working my way toward the door. "The tea is making me feel better already!" I raced to the bus stop before she could make any more helpful suggestions.

24

My day didn't improve at school. Sarah pounced on me the second I stepped off the bus and dragged me to the bathroom before homeroom, her chandelier-like earrings swinging the whole way.

The door closed behind us with a soft *whump!* muffling the noise from the main hall.

"Soooooo?" she said, stretching the word like melty cheese.

"So what?" I replied as innocently as possible. I tugged on my treble clef necklace charm.

"So, about the dance!" she cried. "I was dying to talk to you all weekend but we spent two days on Cape Cod and I couldn't get a second of privacy." She wrinkled her nose. "Spill it."

"Kermit always dances with Miss Piggy." I batted my eyelashes at her, forcing playfulness that I didn't feel. There would be time to tell her about Jake later; I could use this chance to ask her about Punk.

She nudged me. "You are too funny," she said. "But there's something else going on. What's up?" She took a tube of lip gloss from her bag, applied it in the mirror, and handed it to me.

I told her about seeing Punk against the wall after Jake and I finished slow dancing.

"He *must* like you," she said, forehead furrowed while I tried her sparkly gloss. I didn't like its fake pinky shine and wiped it off. Maybe Sarah was right, but that wasn't the vibe I got from him. The first bell rang.

"I dunno," I said, shaking my head. "I'm not sure that's it either." It was nearly time for class, I had no answers, and no idea what to do when I saw either of them.

Sarah leaned back against the sink, her giant purse bumping her knees. "Aren't you going to ask me anything?"

"Huh? Ask you about what?"

"Seriously, Elsie? *Seriously?!* We can have all these conversations about you, you, you, but you never think to ask about who I like or what I'm doing or anything that's going on with me—or anyone else." Her tone shifted faster than a sports car, and I reeled. Where did this come from? What had I done wrong?

Then I remembered our last bathroom chat—and her admonishment to think about other people. Crud.

"Sarah, what? I'm sorry. I didn't know. . . ." I fumbled for the right words. "Is there someone you like?"

Way to sound lame, I chided myself.

Sarah stuffed the lip gloss in her bag and stalked to the door. "Figure it out," she tossed over her shoulder. The door closed. The tardy bell rang.

Fab-tabulous, Elsie.

At least it got Jake and Punk off my mind.

It didn't matter if Jake was in my thoughts or not—he was absent from class and wasn't at lunch. Sarah hadn't spoken to me since we left the bathroom, even though I tried to apologize two more times in the hall, and I was as frayed as an old shoelace.

Hector, who sat between Sarah and me at lunch, hadn't heard from Jake all weekend.

"Did *you*, Elsie?" he asked, mischievous smile dancing at the corners of his lips.

"No," I snapped back. "Why would I?"

The smile disappeared. "Uh, well. Erm. You two . . ."

"We danced. At a *dance*, Hector. You danced too." I couldn't control my words. I knew I was taking a bad few days—and an awful morning—out on him, but I couldn't stop. Or didn't want to.

"You're so darn *touchy*, Elsie. *All the time*," he snapped back at me. He grabbed his bag and gathered his stuff, face red and his eyes bulging behind his glasses. "And you say mean things to me, a lot." He balled his fists. Even his scruffy gray backpack, which had ridden up high on his shoulders, looked angry.

It was like being punctured with a needle. My attitude withered, and I saw—again—what a total jerk I was being. But it was too late. Hector stormed off, the Chewbacca keychain decorating his bag swinging to a furious beat. I'd forgotten—or ignored—everything that Sarah said at the dance about other people's feelings, and for the second time in the same day found myself wishing I could rein in my mouth. Miss Piggy, indeed.

I didn't even need the costume.

I booked it to the girls' bathroom, holding back tears until I was safely in the farthest stall from the door. Once I slid the bolt lock, the flood started. I covered my mouth to trap my sniffles, and just stood there and wept. All I did was hurt my friends—friends I hadn't even realized I *wanted* until joining marching band. Why was I so awful? What was wrong with me? The first bell rang, then the tardy bell. I was late for class, and I didn't care.

I stayed in the bathroom for another ten minutes, and then went to the nurse's office to fake a headache and get a late pass. One of the girls in Hector's section had used that trick to get out of a French test, so I figured it'd work for me. When the nurse saw my blotchy face and swollen eyes, she nearly called my mother. She probably thought I was carrying a contagious disease, not just suffering from bad-frienditis.

Hector and Sarah ignored me in bio, going so far as to switch their seats so we wouldn't be near one another. I totally deserved it. I went through the motions of taking notes and listening while wallowing in my poor behavior.

That afternoon, the band room was its usual chaotic whirl of kids warming up, putting instruments together, and lugging equipment onto the field. I walked through the room in a cloud of shame. My hands skidded off my locker when I went to get my mellophone.

Hector and Sarah stood on the opposite side of the room, speaking quietly to each other, not even glancing in my direction—just like in bio. Steve was busy helping one of the players in the pit pack the marimba, and Punk and AJ pored over a set of drill charts.

Punk! I'd been so upset over the Sarah/Hector thing, I hadn't even thought of him. Great.

I was completely alone in a sea of people.

25

After getting my horn and band buddy, I found a piece of floor away from Hector and Sarah where I wouldn't get trampled and waited, alone. Typically, at the start of practice, we get our instruments and head to sectionals for a quick warm-up, then over to the field for drill and ensemble rehearsal. Today, though, there was a big note on the whiteboard that read: SET UP & SHUT UP.

"Settle down, people! Settle down!" Mr. Sebastian called. A beat. "That means you, drum line! Knock it off back there!" Along with everyone else in the room, I turned to see what Mr. Sebastian was talking about. The drum line had made a human pyramid. The cheers and whoops that exploded—not to mention the theatrical takedown—ate up another minute or two.

"I have some news to share with you. It's exciting, but a bit bittersweet." The overhead lights shined on Mr. Sebastian's receding hairline. He paused. We waited.

"We've been invited to march in the Darcy's Thanksgiving Day parade," he said.

The room erupted louder than a volcano. In fact, I'm sure the people who live *on* the nearest volcano heard us. Mr. Sebastian let us holler for a minute or so, then raised his hands to quiet us down so he could continue. "If we go, we'd travel to New York on the day before Thanksgiving, march in the parade on Thanksgiving morning, and return home late that afternoon. It means you'll be away from your families for the day—"

"My parents can't wait to get rid of me!"

That came from Punk, I'm sure.

"You'll be away from your families for the day," Mr. Sebastian repeated over the laughter. "But I did say there were two parts to this news . . ."

Whispers and murmurs slid around the room like eels through water.

"The bittersweet portion of this is that we've been asked to serve as replacements for the Marching Minutemen."

You could have heard snow fall.

Mr. Sebastian rubbed his face with both hands. "I've spoken with the representative from Darcy's, Mr. Macy, as well as the Minutemen's band director. The Minutemen suggested that we replace them, as a thank-you for the support and help we gave them during the bleacher collapse.

"I know this is an awkward situation," he went on, "and I want you to be the ones to make the final decision. This is a once-in-a-lifetime opportunity for us, but it *is* at the expense of the other band."

AJ raised his hand.

"I think we should do it," he said. "There's no way we'd ever get invited to do the parade if this hadn't happened—we're not big enough to make the minimum size requirement, for starters—and so we seriously should accept the invite or they'll just give it to someone else."

Steve nodded and spoke up. "Maybe there's something we could do to honor them—carry their banner behind ours, or play their marching arrangements?"

His suggestion was met with more chatter, and Mr. Sebastian took an official vote. With all the other arms in the air, no one noticed me, sitting numb, like a block of wood.

I couldn't go to New York for Thanksgiving. There was no way.

The Shining Birches audition was that Saturday.

26

Around me, the excitement built as Mr. Sebastian and AJ ushered us out for practice. We'd have to work our butts off to be ready for national TV on Thanksgiving morning. And parade was not our best skill. Not even close.

Of course, none of that mattered to me. I *had* to be home. Home, practicing for Shining Birches! Sure, much to my surprise I'd grown to like marching band, but I never lost sight of my *real* musical goals: that audition. Despite what I'd told my mother, I was panicked over the lack of time I'd spent behind my horn. Doing quick math, I'd averaged somewhere between five and seven practice hours a week—which was nowhere near what I'd need to master the audition pieces and get into the program. And practicing for Darcy's would mean additional time commitments and a huge distraction. Before the audition, over Thanksgiving break, I'd counted on having two full days of nothing but horn playing (well, and eating). And since my dad was performing in two holiday kickoff concerts, I'd have plenty of home-alone time. With Darcy's in the way, everything would change.

I moved through rehearsal on autopilot, anxiety about Jake (still MIA—was he sick?), Punk, Sarah, and Hector completely overshadowed by New York. I didn't even care when I stepped out of line during the percussion feature, crashed into a piccolo player, and AJ had to stop and reset the band from the beginning.

When we were finally dismissed from the field, I went to the sidelines to find Mr. Sebastian. Anticipating his flip-out, my stomach was as heavy and hard as a rock, but I had to tell him.

He and AJ were leaning over the podium, score for the show stretched out in front of them, working through a section. The other band members were headed into the band room, the pit percussionists wheeling in their instruments.

Finally, they finished. Mr. Sebastian stood straight and AJ folded the long score, then left.

"Um . . . Mr. Sebastian?" My voice was too soft for him to hear. I tried again, louder. "Excuse me?"

He spun around. "Elsie! What can I do for you, dear?"

His smile was so wide and kind that I froze. I didn't know how to begin. To my complete humiliation, my eyes filled with tears.

"It's . . . uhh . . . well . . ." I had to force the words out. "I just can't go to New York," I said, rushing everything together. "I'm sorry."

His smile melted faster than ice cream on a hot day.

"What do you mean, Elsie?" he asked. "I realize that students haven't spoken with their parents yet, so there may be some conflicts. Were you planning on traveling for the holiday?"

I wished it was that easy.

"Not exactly," I said. My hands were sweaty against the cold metal of the mellophone. "I have a big audition on Saturday."

"Saturday?"

I nodded.

"As in, two days after the parade?"

I nodded again.

"Well," he went on, big smile back, "that's no problem! We'll be back on Thursday evening . . . in plenty of time for your audition."

How was I going to say this without sounding snotty and ridiculous?

"I understood which day we're coming back," I said. "That has nothing to do with it. I just need the practice time."

It sounded snotty and ridiculous.

Mr. Sebastian's face twitched.

"Are you saying that you are forgoing a major performance opportunity to rehearse?" There was heavy silence while he waited for my reply.

"Kind of?" I offered. "But not really." Getting out of quicksand would be easier than getting out of this mess. "I'm sorry, Mr. Sebastian, I just really, really need to practice."

He inhaled through his nose in a noisy huff, then tilted his head to watch a flock of birds. The field was empty, and in the parking lot, a few cars started as kids left.

"I gather this is an important audition for you," he said. His words came out carefully formed, with distinct spaces between them, like glass marbles.

I nodded. "It's for Shining Birches."

Mr. Sebastian took off his glasses and rubbed his face. I couldn't tell if he was completely frustrated or furious.

"Elsie, that's a program for upperclassmen. Most of the applicants—"

"I know." I cut him off, surprising myself. But I really, really didn't want to hear him talk about how young I was, or how I probably wouldn't get in, or how it'd be better if I waited until next year to audition. Heard enough of that lately, thank you very much.

"I know a lot about the program already," I said, trying to cover up my rudeness. "My dad went there when he was in high school, and I know how hard it is to get in—especially for someone my age. That's why I need to practice."

Mr. Sebastian rubbed his face again and pinched the bridge of his nose. He took another deep breath. "Let's go into my office," he said.

I followed him across the field into the nearly empty band room. AJ was there, watching a recording of our parade performance the day of the Minutemen bleacher collapse. He barely glanced at us as we entered—he was too busy scribbling notes on a sheet of legal paper.

Mr. Sebastian pulled a ring of keys from his pocket and opened his office. I hadn't been in there before, and was surprised at how small and cluttered it was. Shelves of videotapes, music scores, drill chart folders, and books overflowed onto the floor. Photos of the Hellcats going back to 1995 lined the walls, and instruments needing repairs nestled in cases labeled with yellow tags formed a shaky pyramid on the floor. There was barely room for a chair opposite his desk.

"Have a seat," he said.

"Look, Elsie," he went on when I had settled myself, mellophone balanced across my lap, "I don't know why you want to rush into Shining Birches, but I can appreciate your work ethic."

I waited.

"Perhaps there's a way we can work this out and get everyone's needs met."

"What do you mean?"

"You need to practice, I need—and I think *you* need—

to come to New York. You're the strongest player in your section—not to mention the loudest—and if we do end up adopting the Minutemen's parade music, there's potential for a major mellophone solo in the piece. We need your chops."

A major mellophone solo? That was intriguing, as was his comment that he thought I needed to travel with the group. What was that supposed to mean?

"What if we arranged it so that you could use the band room at lunch and after school for some extra practice time between now and then. Would that help?"

I considered his offer. I'd practiced during my lunch period all through eighth grade, but that was because I hadn't had anyone to eat lunch *with*. Then again, since Hector and Sarah weren't speaking to me, and who knew what was going on with Jake, it was kind of perfect. And, although I hated to admit it, the promise of a solo at Darcy's—in front of a national TV audience—made the parade sound less like a distraction and more like an amazing performance opportunity. But could I handle both?

"Practicing in the band room would definitely help, but I need to think about everything, Mr. Sebastian. Is that okay?" I hated not being able to jump up and down, hug him and shout "Yes!"—because, based on the look on his face, that's what he was expecting—but I had to be honest. Marching band was not the most important thing in the world to me: horn was. And if I'd learned anything this season, it was that they were two great things that didn't go together.

When I left his office a few minutes later, I was smiling and feeling a little bit better about the New York situation. Of course, by the time I reached the sidewalk, everything else came flooding back.

Bye-bye, good mood.

27

Wrapped in a fog of worry, I went home wishing there was someone I could talk to about my Darcy's/Shining Birches dilemma. Although, I thought ruefully, if I hadn't caused Hector/Sarah and Punk dilemmas, I would have *lots* of someones to discuss it with. And then there was Jake. I wasn't sure that was a dilemma, yet, but it definitely was . . . something. At this point, regardless of what happened at the dance, he was the only person who was still speaking to me. At least, I hoped he was.

When I got home, I opened a blank e-mail and plugged in Jake's address. What to say? "Hey—how are you? Where were you today? I messed up with nearly everyone else and I need advice about my horn." Lame. The blank message block didn't offer any better suggestions, so I spent about fifteen minutes typing his address in the SEND field, thinking awhile, then erasing it. I did the same thing on his FriendPage. A few people had left posts about the dance, and there were about ten posts asking where he was today, but he hadn't responded. He must be really sick or something.

I couldn't come up with anything to put on his wall either, so after checking Punk's, Hector's, and Sarah's pages—all of which were dotted with messages about the upcoming trip to New York, and none of them had left notes on mine—I just logged off and dragged out my homework, depressed over the whole situation.

At dinner, I picked at my food. I kept wondering how to bring up the whole "I'm going to miss Thanksgiving for a marching band gig" thing. I mean, if I told my parents I was going to be playing in a symphony, it'd be one thing, but I didn't know how they'd take me promenading through Manhattan with my instrument. Not to mention their reaction to the whole "cutting into my Shining Birches practice time" thing too. At one point, Mom told a supposedly funny story about a dye pack at the bank accidentally exploding on a teller. Dad laughed, but I was so wrapped up in my own world, I missed the humor.

When he stopped laughing, both of them turned to me, like I was supposed to say something next. Realizing that made me even less interested in telling them.

"Uh, so," I started. "The, uh, marching band got some great news today." I stabbed a clump of ziti with my fork, paying precise attention to each strand of cheese that stretched off the plate.

"What kind of news?" My dad's fork hit his plate with a *clink!* I dotted my pasta around, gathering extra sauce.

"We've been invited to march in the Darcy's Thanksgiving parade," I blurted, then stuffed the sauce-filled glob into my mouth. I was so nervous, it tasted like cardboard. I choked it down.

"Pretty exciting, but isn't that short notice?" my dad asked. Sometimes, I hated that he knew so much about music. "They usually issue invitations in late September."

"That *is* exciting," Mom echoed. "And a long way to go by yourself."

I reminded them about the bleachers collapse (ignoring Mom's cringes), summarizing how we came to be invited in the Minutemen's place. The whole time, Mom and Dad were practicing their psychic parenting skills. There was even a forehead argument at one point, where dad furrowed his whole brow and raised one eyebrow. Mom shook her head at him, tilted her head toward me, and shook it. Dad raised both eyebrows in response.

"So we just found out today," I finished. I speared a meatball and ate it whole, hoping to prevent discussion. "Oh," I added, trying to sneak in the information as an afterthought, "I might be playing a major solo too."

"What about Shining Birches?" Of course that'd be the next thing out of Dad's mouth. Even though it was the first thing that occurred to me, coming from him it was totally annoying.

"Mr. Sebastian will let me use the band room during lunch for extra practice, and I'll work out a plan with Mr. Rinaldi," I responded as if I had it under control. "I'm in good shape anyway." I crossed my fingers after that one.

Dad whistled low, through his teeth.

"Are you sure it's a good idea to accept that solo if they offer it?" he asked.

"What?!" He thought I should turn it *down*?!

"Well, I haven't heard you play your audition pieces lately, and the last time I did, you needed substantial help. Are you sure you'll be ready, especially once you add practices for another solo into your schedule?"

Dad, on repeat. I opened and closed my mouth, trying to rein in my anger.

"Of *course* I'll be ready!" I snipped. I'll just have to sacrifice time with the few friends I have left, a part of me whispered. I ignored that part. Before I could go on, my mom spoke up.

"You'll miss Thanksgiving dinner at Aunt Denise's."

Aunt Denise's Thanksgivings flashed through my head: dry turkey, younger cousins running around, trying to blow up the turkey carcass using illegal firecrackers that Uncle Rick stashed in the garage after the Fourth of July. Nope, I wouldn't be missing anything. "Well, you can watch me on TV," I said through clenched teeth.

Mom leaned over her plate, toward me. "New York is a dangerous place, and I don't like knowing that you'll be running around unsupervised. Are you taking buses up and back?"

I rolled my eyes. "Mom, we'll be supervised. It's not like I'm going to leave parade formation to go sightseeing and come back and get back in line! Give me a *break*." I took a breath. "You might not like it, but you have to let me go."

"Elsie, we're just concerned about you." My mom was trying to defuse the situation, but I wouldn't have it. I was sick of feeling bad about my choices, what I said, or the decisions I made—with my parents *and* my friends. This was my choice. I owned it.

I pushed back from the table and glared at my parents. "I'm playing. I'm going. Deal with it."

I marched up to my room, slamming the door behind me.

28

I hid in my room for the rest of the night, rejecting my mother's two attempts to talk.

"Leave me *alone*!" I called from the bed. My dad never checked on me.

A major problem came with my self-imposed exile: I had nowhere to practice. I couldn't leave, which was my original plan, because to leave I'd have to get dropped off somewhere. And it was a Monday night, which meant no symphony gigs for my dad. But now more than ever, I needed to practice for the audition and prep for my lesson.

Tormented by my own stupidity, I set up my music stand and put my horn together. I blew warm air through it while I considered my options. I had to play; I had no choice. But I didn't want to give my dad the satisfaction of hearing me run through the pieces after my dinner table explosion. I stared at the "Music washes away from the soul the dust of everyday life" quote that I'd plastered across the top of my mirror. My soul was definitely dusty.

I *needed* to play.

But how?

Then it occurred to me: my practice mute! I had one stuffed in the back of my closet, but never used it—I couldn't work on tone with it in.

"Should we try it?" I asked my horn. I dug it out, stuffed it into the bell, and *voila!* my formerly mellow-brassy sound was reduced to a teeny honking. I also cut my air, playing as quietly as possible—the antithesis of my marching band blowouts.

"Perfect!" I said aloud. If it had hands, I'd've slapped my horn a high five.

I played for two hours, softly pouring my frustration and anger into the instrument, working through the audition pieces and dusting my soul. There were just over three weeks to perfect them, and if all of my practice sessions went this well, I'd blow the judges' hair back.

Maybe all I needed to do between now and then was stay this miserable?

The next morning, I rushed through my routine to avoid conversation with my mom and dad. Leaving the house was no help, though—the walk to the bus stop just brought me closer to the mess that waited for me at school. I'd have to talk to Jake. Hector and Sarah too.

And probably Punk. I nearly groaned out loud.

I arrived at school a wreck. The nervous-excited (Jake), nervous-shameful (Hector/Sarah), and nervous-nervous (Punk) feelings wreaked havoc on my stomach and palms. They were sweating so much they left little pools on the green vinyl bus seat, and I couldn't breathe without wanting to hurl.

I saw Jake first. He was standing next to my locker, a guarded look on his face, hands in his pockets.

"Hey," he said.

"Hey," I said in response, hoping that it came out sounding cooler than I felt. He moved aside. My hands trembled so much I could barely spin the locker's combination dial. "Were you sick?"

"Nope," he said, hair flopping into his eyes. His voice made the hair on the back of my neck stand up and sent a tickle down my back. I tried to hide the damp handprints plastered on my textbooks as I shoved them into my bag. "My dad's aunt died, so we had to go to New York on short notice. The funeral was yesterday."

I hadn't expected that. "Oh." What else should I say? "I'm sorry."

We fell into step, my heart slamming. He was walking me to homeroom!

"Thanks. I didn't exactly know her—I hadn't seen her since I was little. She was old and pretty sick. My dad was bummed out about it."

I nodded like I knew what that was like. No one in my family had died—I still had all four grandparents—and I'd never been to a funeral. They seemed scary.

"Well, I'm glad you're okay." We'd reached the door to my homeroom and the first bell buzzed. "You're going to be late."

"I'll run." The girl who sat in front of me pushed between us to get into class. Jake kicked at the door frame with the toe of his shoe. "Look, Elsie, I talked to Hector last night. He's pretty ticked. So's Sarah."

A pang of jealousy hit me—he talked to them last night, but not me? But after the way I'd behaved, why would he want to talk to me at all? I felt as big as the spider crawling across the industrial tile floor.

"You've gotta talk to them."

I nodded. He waited, probably thinking I'd say something else. But I didn't know what to say. I'd messed up, and I couldn't blame them for not wanting to give me another chance.

"Okay, then," Jake said, giving up on me responding. "I'll see you later."

Reluctantly, I brought my eyes up to his. He was staring straight at me, totally serious, jaw set. Then his face broke into a blinding smile that melted my insides and made me grateful that I hadn't ticked him off too. Yet. He jogged away.

In a daze, a zombie chicken for sure, I went into the

classroom and took my seat. He hadn't said anything about the dance, but his smile and walk to homeroom were indicators that something had happened, that things had changed between us. But how? And did I want them to? The hair on the back of my neck stood up again, and I realized that maybe I did. Okay, I definitely did.

While the morning announcements blared over the PA system, I thought about how to handle Hector. He was right—I was mean to him a lot, and not because I didn't like him. He just was in the wrong place at the wrong time, saying the wrong thing. None of that was his fault. It was my fault that my brain and mouth didn't get along. I was too quick to judge.

And Sarah was right too—I never asked her anything about *her*. To be honest, I never asked about *anyone* else because I was always so wrapped up in Elsie-land. I sighed. The bell rang.

They deserved big, big apologies when I saw them.

And that didn't take long. On my way to class, I spotted Hector and Sarah standing in the hall, talking. Lump in my throat, I walked over to them. Sarah nudged Hector, who turned to watch me. He was wearing his "Han shot first" T-shirt. He frowned, and although I couldn't see his eyes behind his glasses, I was sure they were hard.

"Hector," I began gently, "I'm really, really—"

"Save it, Elsie," Sarah snapped. "You've apologized to him—us—before. It doesn't mean you're going to change.

You're still the same obnoxious kid you were in junior high, always acting better than everyone else because you play the horn."

Her sharp words took my breath away. Heat rose in my face. Hector shifted from foot to foot, caught between the two of us.

"I know," I tried. "But this time—"

"This time is different?" said Hector, voice sad. "I don't know if I believe you, Elsie." The first bell buzzed.

"I don't," Sarah snipped.

They weren't even giving me a chance to *explain*!

"Look, I know we're not as important as your *goals* or your *horn*, so we'll let you get to class," Sarah said.

As much as her words hurt, they also showed me her point. As soon as horn life got stressful, I treated them poorly. I was so embarrassed, I didn't say anything in response, just watched helplessly as they left me standing in the hall and the crowd thinned.

I didn't even try to make it to English on time. The late bell rang when I was just steps from the door, and I had nothing to say to Mrs. Beman when she told me I'd be getting a tardy for the period.

I saw Jake outside of history, just before lunch. Based on his expression, he knew what went on between me, Hector, and Sarah in the hall.

"Look, Elsie," he said before the bell, "they're upset."

"I *know* they're upset! I'm upset too! It's my fault that

they're so mad." I was dangerously close to losing control.

"I don't want to be in the middle of this," he said. "I can't be. You have to work it out with them, Elsie."

Miserable, I nodded. What was I going to do at lunch? I didn't want to sit there while Hector and Sarah threw eye-daggers at me. I wanted to escape behind my horn.

When class ended, I met Jake in the hall. "Go to lunch with those guys. I think they need time to cool off and I don't want to make things all weird."

Confusion flitted across Jake's face. "What about you?"

"I'm going to the band room," I said. "I need to practice."

"Elsie!" Jake rubbed his head with both hands. "Seriously, is that the best idea?"

"Well, they don't want to talk to me right now," I said. "And playing will make me feel better. Honest."

Jake just shook his head. "Suit yourself."

"I'll see you later, okay?" I didn't want him to be mad at me too, but this was the best I could do. And despite what he thought, I wasn't hiding. Playing would hopefully help me get my emotions in order.

"Fine. I'll come by your locker at the end of the day." We stood awkwardly. What should I do? Hug him?

Instead of a hug, he squeezed my hand.

"See ya," he said, and left me in the middle of the hall, alone.

29

I spent all of lunch blowing my brains out on my horn, working those audition pieces like it was my job. (Okay, it was.)

And like I'd told Jake, it made me feel better—for the time being. However, after I put my horn away, I realized that it didn't magically fix my friend situation. I trudged to bio, mentally running through scenarios for apologies and making up. I was no good at this stuff, and my guts churned to an andante beat.

The Sarah/Hector wall was back. I tried to break through it with a smile when I came in, but they turned away, eyes dark.

I dropped my book bag on the floor and slumped in my chair. They were not about to make this easy.

"Look, guys," I whispered at their backs, while the teacher took attendance. "I'm sorry. I'm *really* sorry."

Nothing. No reaction. I may as well not have been there.

"Can't we at least talk about this?" I tried.

The girl in front of me snickered. I wanted to poke her neck with my pencil, but I refrained.

Hector peered at me out of the corner of his eye, then frowned.

Mr. O'Malley brought the class to order, forcing me to stop my ineffective apologizing. I took notes, sneaking glances at Sarah and Hector the whole time he was lecturing on cell structure. Maybe they'd thaw a little, so that when it was time for us to break into lab groups, I could partner with them.

"Okay, get in your groups!" Mr. O'Malley called.

I turned to Sarah and Hector. They weren't looking at me at all. Without saying anything, they got up and walked to a table in the far corner of the room, joining a girl from color guard and someone I didn't know.

"You can totally work with us, Elise!" the girl in front of me chirped.

"It's *Elsie*," I snapped as I gathered my lab sheets. My sharp tone didn't even come close to the stabbing pain I felt as Hector and Sarah went to work without me.

The following afternoon, Sarah and Hector still weren't speaking to me. Jake, maintaining his neutrality, insisted that the three of us leave him out of it—which basically left me out of lunch. Again. Why sit at the table and make it awkward for everyone? I practiced. Again.

Having no friends meant I had nothing to lose, so I decided to confront Punk at practice to figure out what his deal was. I hadn't seen him in the halls, and he was purposely avoiding me at band—every time I turned to him, he made sure to be absorbed in something else.

But our usual practice schedule had changed. Everyone was getting their instruments and then sitting on the risers, not heading straight for sectionals. I retrieved my mellophone from my locker and plunked down next to Jake. Hector and Sarah stayed on the opposite side of the room, as cold as the Arctic. Jake gave me a warm smile and squeezed my hand, which tingled like an electric shock.

"Who's that?" someone behind me whispered. I'd been so busy staring at Jake, I hadn't paid attention to much else. And I definitely hadn't noticed the guy hunched over the podium with AJ and Mr. Sebastian. They were all studying a score.

Mr. Sebastian called us to order, and the other kid straightened. He had one arm in a sling. And that's when I realized: He was a Marching Minuteman.

"This is Kip Bellsworth, drum major for Revolutionary High's band," Mr. Sebastian announced. "He's going to work with us to help us prepare for our Darcy's parade debut." Mr. Sebastian said a bunch of other stuff, but I didn't listen.

Instead, I focused on Kip, who was tall and cute—was that a requirement for being drum major?—then I flashed back to the day of the accident, remembering his intense eyes and the talk about how he made his band run laps before practice. The intensity had left his face. All that was left was sadness. Where had he been when the collapse happened? The accident was a month ago, and since he was still bandaged, I guessed he'd gotten pretty hurt. And in spite of that he was here to help us out.

"This is a big deal," Jake whispered. "This doesn't usually happen."

I would guess not. And from Kip's expression—a mix of worried, disappointed, and determined—this was a *very* big deal to him. I'm sure he wished he were working with the Minutemen.

Mr. Sebastian sent us out with our section leaders to learn the new parade piece. I was so nervous about confronting Punk—who'd been sitting on the opposite side of the room—I didn't hear Mr. Sebastian calling my name until Jake nudged me.

"If you have a minute, Elsie?" Mr. Sebastian said. He blew a big, exasperated puff of air from his cheeks. "You'll catch up with the high brass momentarily."

The other drum major, Kip, still stood with Mr. Sebastian. Up close, I could see the faint yellow bruises around one eye. His arm was wrapped in a cast to the elbow. And I noticed that I'd been mistaken earlier. The intensity was still on his face. In fact, he studied me like he was evaluating my worthiness for whatever they had planned.

Immediately, I stood taller. Not that it helped much.

"The Minutemen's parade medley contains the piccolo solo from Sousa's 'Stars and Stripes Forever.' I assume you're familiar with it?" Mr. Sebastian asked. I nodded. Of course I was. It was the last song played at every Boston Pops concert! I'd heard its frolicking *tweet-tweet, tweet-tweet, tweedle-leedle-leet-deet, leedle-leedle-eet-leet-lee!* since I was a baby.

Kip crossed his good arm over his bad one. "We rearranged the solo for mello in our band," he said. "We have a kickin' player and thought it would get more attention that way." He shrugged. "Plus, it'd be easier than mike-ing a flute or pic at the parade."

"Okay," I said, keeping cool. I hoped I knew where this was going.

Kip and Mr. Sebastian exchanged glances.

"I want to offer it to you," Mr. Sebastian said. "You're the loudest player in your section, and I'm confident you can master it. Can you handle learning it and your audition pieces for Shining Birches?"

Kip showed nothing but skepticism. Just another person to add to my list to prove wrong.

"I can absolutely handle it," I said, while my brain replayed my dad saying that I shouldn't accept the solo if they offered it to me. "I'll totally do it," I added, sealing the deal for myself.

"Sure you're up for it?" Kip asked me. His eyes searched

my face. I'm sure he saw what everyone else did: a short, round freshman who looked like she belonged in junior high. And that was not me—not anymore.

"Don't worry what I'm up for," I snapped. "I will rock that solo harder than you could ever dream." *That* made Kip take a step back—and sparked admiration in his eyes.

"Easy, there," Mr. Sebastian cautioned. "Okay. You'll get it next practice. Go to sectionals."

I felt Kip's skeptical eyes on me as I left. Sure, it'd mean practicing a little more on mello than I'd planned, but the solo was only a few bars. Once I had it memorized, I'd be golden.

30

I joined the rest of my section in our customary practice spot by the oak tree. Only now, instead of blazing summer heat, a chill autumn breeze blew by, kicking up fallen leaves and swirling them in a ballet around our ankles. Punk stood between two other players, not in his usual spot on the end, next to me. He didn't look at me as I joined the group.

Steve ran us through the march medley once or twice. In most Sousa marches, the trombones carry the melody—the main part of the song—so other instruments just play off-beats underneath them. As a high brass player, all I had to worry about was not getting lost while counting. And since I can count to two, I was set.

But Steve wanted to make sure we stayed together, hit the notes cleanly, and got through the piece without crashing and burning. The medley began with "The Liberty Bell" (which, Steve told us, was also the theme from some ancient TV show called *Monty Python's Flying Circus*—okay, he didn't say "ancient," he said "awesome," but who cares?), went into the "Washington Post" march, and finished with "Stars and Stripes Forever."

"Okay, time's up!" Steve said. "Head to ensemble."

We gathered our stuff. This was my chance to talk to Punk. I sidled up to him as he cleared the spit valve from his horn. I coughed.

"Hey." He glanced at me, but didn't say anything.

"Uh, look," I tried, shuffling my feet so I was slightly in front of him, forcing him to watch me. "I know you're mad. Or upset. Actually, I don't know what you are—only that you danced with me when you were Frankenstein and we haven't talked since." The words tumbled out of me like a swift horn run.

Punk raised a pierced eyebrow. We were close to the ensemble arc. I didn't have much time.

"I'm not sure what I did, but I'm sorry for it. And if you tell me what the problem is, maybe I can fix it." I felt like a tiny dog yapping for attention.

He tilted his head to the sky and blew a big puff of air out of his cheeks, just like Mr. Sebastian had. "Chicken, it's all cool. Seriously."

"Oh, really?" I said. The Sahara wasn't as dry as my voice. "That's great."

We'd reached ensemble. Kip and AJ stood at the podium, conferring.

Punk stepped into the mellophone line between two other players. No way was he freezing me out like Sarah and Hector. I needed to know what was going on. Jutting my elbows, I muscled in between Punk and Mac, another junior.

"A little 'excuse me' would go a long way, Zombie-chick," Mac snapped.

"Sorry," I said. Punk raised that eyebrow again. AJ called us to attention.

"I want an *answer*," I whispered at Punk out of the corner of my mouth. I set my gaze on Kip and AJ.

"There is none," he muttered. "We're cool. That's it!"

AJ counted off, and we played the medley. When we reached the solo section in "Stars and Stripes" the rest of the band rested or played off-beats. I imagined playing the intricate solo, lighter than what's typically played on a brass instrument, and fairly complex. It'd be awesome.

However, realizing the amount of work it would take to perfect this and my audition pieces terrified me. Now I understood why Dad said not to take it. But I couldn't resist the opportunity. I pushed my nerves down.

We finished the run-through and AJ put us in parade rest.

"Not bad for a first time," he called.

"But not great either," Kip added. He paced back and forth in front of the podium. "The key to making this medley work is articulating every note—really making them pop—and right now, they're running together like mush."

"Possibly because it's the first time we've *played* it," I muttered, louder than I probably should have. Who was he to diss our articulation?

"What was that?" AJ's head snapped in my direction. "Who said that? You are in parade rest, and there is *no talking*!" He came to our side of the field. "I know it came from over here."

That's when I realized I was in trouble. AJ was mad that someone had spoken while Kip was talking—it totally made AJ, and our band, look bad. So much for using my brain more than my mouth. I swallowed hard.

"So?" AJ said. "Who's running laps?"

I swallowed again. Next to me, Punk shifted. I stepped out of line.

"It was me," I said, owning up to the comment. "I said it."

Over AJ's shoulder, Kip shook his head. And here's another reason for him to love giving me the solo, I thought.

"Four laps, Chicken," AJ growled, eyes narrowed behind his sunglasses. "*Run!*"

Obediently, I jogged to the sideline, everyone staring at me the entire time, embarrassed, yeah, but also proud that I was taking responsibility for what I'd done, instead of Punk going in my place. My mellophone safely on the ground by the thirty yard line, I took a breath and began my laps.

As much as I hated running, all of the marching and playing must have built up my stamina, because it didn't feel as awful as it would have three months ago. I let my legs carry me around the track while my brain floated through all that had happened recently. Even though things were bad with Hector, Sarah, and Punk, I hoped I could make the changes I needed to, to be a better friend and straighten things out between us. By the time I finished my first lap the band was rehearsing again, the Sousa marches and spinning flags providing the backdrop for my "punishment."

After my fourth lap, I was just a little out of breath. I grabbed my instrument and returned to my spot. On the way, I met Punk's eyes. He grinned at me from behind his horn. I snuck looks at him every so often while we played, until he bumped me with his hip to knock it off. I grinned, but caught Jake frowning behind his trumpet. Had he seen? Did he care?

We finished rehearsing—Kip making us play "The Liberty Bell" section so many times I could do it in my sleep—and I turned to Punk.

"So what's the deal?" I asked on our walk back to the band room. Jake, ahead of us, turned around, saw Punk and me, and kept going.

"Straight up?" He rolled the stud under his lower lip with two fingers. His hair was dyed blue today.

"Yeah. Straight up."

He sighed. "You remind me of someone," he said, eyes on the ground.

"Someone . . . ?" I repeated.

"Yeah." He stopped walking and shifted from foot to foot. "Me." He fiddled with the lip stud again.

"I remind you of you?" I asked, trying to sort things out. "Which is why you covered for me those times, walked me to French, and danced with me at the dance?" Punk was weirder than I thought.

"Yeah. Me—a little young, a lot of attitude, and not a lot of brains." He grinned. "My big brother kept an eye out for me freshman year, so I thought I'd do the same for you."

"Paying it forward?" I asked. We'd stopped just outside of the band room.

"Kinda. Or karma . . . whatever. But you're a pain and make it hard."

"Oh, thanks," I said, oozing sarcasm. "You have to *earn* your karma points with me."

"Sometimes people do things because they're trying to be *nice*, not for any other reason, Elsie. You know . . . *niiiice*?" He drew the word out and cocked his head. Odd as he was, Punk meant what he said. He'd been trying to help me, and I'd been searching for ulterior motives. Put another tick mark in the "Elsie is an idiot" column.

"Nice," I repeated. "*Nice*. I may have heard that word once or twice." I reached up and gave him a big hug, grateful that we were back on good terms. "Thanks for watching out for me," I said, adding Punk to my list of people to treat better. "I've kind of always wanted a blue-haired, facially decorated sibling."

He patted my head. "At your service, petit poulet."

Talking with Punk gave me hope that I could fix things with Sarah and Hector, if they'd give me the chance. Back in the band room, I whistled a strain from "Ode to Joy" while packing up my mellophone and gathering my stuff. When I turned around, I spotted Jake at his locker, back to me. I went over to say good-bye.

"Hey," I said. Talking to him still made me feel awkward, giddy, and zingy all at the same time, like I was on the verge of doing something out of control. I liked the feeling, but it also freaked me out a little. Same with his smile—I'd see it, and couldn't remember what I wanted to say, but I didn't care.

But when Jake turned around, there was no smile on his face. There was no expression there at all, actually, just a guarded look in his eye.

"Hey," he said, and went back to wiping down his trumpet.

So surprised by his anti-Jake greeting, I took a step back.

"Is, uhhh . . . everything okay?" I stammered, wondering if I'd imagined everything—the dance, the squeezed hands, the smiles, the escorts to class.

Jake folded up the dingy gray cleaning cloth and stuck it in his locker, keeping his attention on exactly what he was doing.

"I dunno," he finally said. "You tell me."

I had no idea what he was talking about. Without even knowing what the deal was, my eyes started to tear up.

"Tell you what?" I said. I tried to sound tough, to cover my struggle against tears.

His locker clicked shut. He turned to me. His mouth was in a tight line and his forehead furrowed. Even his hair, typically flopping over his eyes, seemed sad.

"Seriously, Elsie? What's your deal?"

I had no idea what he was talking about. The band room had nearly emptied, and I knew I'd have to leave soon to catch the late bus home.

"My *deal*?" I repeated. "I have no deal." There was an edge to my voice. I hadn't done anything to Jake! Why was he being like this for no reason?

"Okay," he said, and crossed his arms. "Fine. Maybe *you* don't have a deal; does Punk?"

"Huh?" was what came out of my mouth, but what ran through my brain were the times that Punk had helped me out, covered for me in band, the Halloween dance, and, finally, today, me pursuing him around the field to get him to talk to me. In that instant, I saw what it probably looked like to Jake—that I liked Punk, not him, or that I was playing some sort of game.

Unfortunately, in the seconds that it took me to put everything together, Jake had turned away again, this time heading for the door. Me not saying anything was probably all he needed to hear.

"There is no deal," I said, going after him.

"What is it, then?" he said. We were in the hall now, heading to the buses. Jake walked with stiff legs, hurt and anger trailing behind him.

"It's just . . ." I trailed off, not sure how to explain things with Punk in the remaining steps to the bus. "He's just looking out for me," I tried. "That's all."

Jake shook his head slightly. "That's all?" It came out sarcastic.

Inside, my emotions raced—angry, hurt, and embarrassed competed for the win.

"That's all," I said, hurt winning. The tears I'd been fighting spilled over and I swiped my eyes. "He's a *friend*."

We'd reached the buses. Jake stopped and faced me. I saw how upset he was, but I needed him to see that I was too.

Drained and exhausted from apologizing to everyone all day, "I'm sorry," was all I could offer.

"Me too," he said, and climbed onto his bus.

I watched his—and then mine—pull away from the curb. And I cried for the entire long walk home.

31

I saw the next few days through a near-constant blur of tears. Hector and Sarah were still ignoring me. Jake was still upset about the Punk thing, and although we'd spoken once or twice before history class, he stopped coming to my locker and I couldn't remember the last time I'd seen one of his big smiles.

So I did what I do best: hole up and practice, practice, practice the bad feelings away. If I wasn't playing Brahms on my horn, the rewritten Sousa solo was coming out of my mellophone. Thanks to my less-than-stellar mental state, both sounded like funeral dirges.

I came home on Tuesday afternoon, two weeks before Thanksgiving, to find my dad sitting at the table, a grim look on his face. Well, the grim look had been there ever since I told him I had taken the New York solo. It was just *more* grim, if that was even possible.

"What's up? You ready?" I dropped my backpack on

the floor and headed to the fridge. He was supposed to take me to Mr. Rinaldi's. "My lesson's in thirty minutes. Can you still drop me off?"

"Mr. Rinaldi just called," Dad said. He took off his glasses and rubbed his face. "He had to cancel your lesson today."

Halfway in the fridge, my hand wrapped around a package of cheese sticks, I couldn't move. "What?" I asked. I stayed that way, hoping I'd misheard my father.

"He had to cancel. There's been a family emergency."

I left the cheese sticks where they were, straightened, and closed the door.

"What?!"

"His wife is in the hospital. She may have had a stroke. It's serious, Elsie."

I felt terrible for Mr. Rinaldi. Mrs. Rinaldi was so nice— she always checked in on my lesson and complimented my playing. I hoped she was okay, but I needed my lessons! My feelings fizzled and popped like hot oil.

Everything I'd been holding together—the crazy practice schedule, the stress over Shining Birches and the new solo, the Hector/Sarah drama, and the Jake fight—came bubbling to the surface. This could not be happening. I *needed* Mr. Rinaldi—he played principal horn for the Boston Symphony before my dad took the job, he served on the faculty of Shining Birches for the past ten years, and last year sat on the audition panel. He knew what they wanted—and knew how to make sure I *became* what they wanted. I rested my head against the fridge door and fought tears.

"Unfortunately there's nothing we can do," my dad said calmly, seeming oblivious to my impending mental collapse. "These things happen."

"No, it's more than *unfortunate*," I spat. "It's TERRIBLE! What am I going to do, find another horn teacher in—oh, twenty-eight minutes?" I squeezed my hands into fists and stuffed them into my pockets.

"Look, Elsie, I know this is a disappointment," he began, "but maybe it's also a sign that this is something you're not ready to take on. You have enough on your plate with traveling to New York for your other group. You can apply again next year."

I stared at him, disbelieving. How could he say that to me? "You are asking me to *give up*?! Are you *kidding*? I have worked so, so hard for this, Dad! You know that!"

He pinched the bridge of his nose—his "it's hard to deal with a teenage girl" gesture.

"Look, honey, I'm not sure *how* hard you've worked or how much you want this. You never practice when I'm home. You never ask me for help. The one time I did help you earlier this fall, you shooed me out of your room like I was an unwanted visitor. You spend all of your time with marching band, not even playing the instrument you claim to love. What am I *supposed* to think?"

His words ripped a ragged wound across my heart. I couldn't even breathe, let alone talk. *This* was how he really felt? That I wasn't doing enough, didn't love my instrument enough, that I wasn't practicing enough? I'd had my suspicions, but the truth burned in a way I was completely unprepared for.

"I joined marching band because I needed another ensemble for Shining Birches after missing Boston Youth Orchestra for our 'family vacation,'" I reminded him through gritted teeth. "I'm sorry that I ended up *liking* a non-orchestral group!" It was the first time I admitted that out loud, and even though I was in a haze of fury and hurt, I still experienced a twinge of surprise at the admission.

"And I HAVE been practicing. Just not around *you*! Around people who support me and believe I'm *actually a good player*!" That last part emerged as nearly a scream. I couldn't take it anymore. I launched myself off the front of the fridge with one foot, passed my dad's stunned expression, and raced upstairs to my bedroom, where I slammed the door as hard as I could.

I threw myself on the bed and screamed into a pillow, kicking my feet on the mattress like a kid tempertantruming in the grocery store. Fury raged through me. I couldn't believe how my dad had just cut me down. He had *no idea* what I was going through to prepare for Shining Birches! I'd turned down invitations to hang out with my friends, gotten into fights with them over how much I played—and now maybe lost all of them because of my horn-first thinking—and still did my schoolwork and practiced constantly. All because I wanted to be like him, do what he did!

I hopped off my bed and paced around my room, twisting the pillow in my hands. I needed to release the tension and anger that rolled through my body. My horn was downstairs by the back door—but there was no way I was going to go get it. I kept pacing and wrecking that pillow, half expecting my dad to come to the door and definitely not wanting him to.

He never came.

After about a half hour of walking back and forth, my fury level dropped from Thunderous Rage to Smoldering Anger. I sat on the bed. And as soon as I did, the scene downstairs started to replay itself in my mind. I stood and pushed it away. Yes, I was abominably angry, but I had another problem: no horn teacher. That had to be my first priority—*had* to be, especially after the argument I'd just had.

And after that argument, there was no way I'd ask my dad—or any of his friends—for help. Ever.

After a quick internal debate—to ask for help, or not to ask for help, that is the question—I decided to see if anyone who was still speaking to me could offer some guidance. Or, at least, moral support. I quietly crept out of my room and woke up the computer—why Mom insisted on leaving it out in the open if she was never around to check on where my virtual self was lurking was beyond me—not wanting my dad to hear me and start round two. Almost as soon as I logged on, the chat bubble popped up on my screen. Hector, Steve, and Jake were online. So was Punk.

BigHorn_211: yo
The_Jaker: hey

"ChewbaccaRulez"—Hector's screen name, stayed silent. I had a another internal debate over what Jake's "hey" meant—did he finally believe me about Punk? Was he just being polite?—but then brought my attention back to my horn problem. Instead of getting into it with all the guys, I told Jake I'd see him tomorrow and sent Punk a private message to ask if we could talk.

Itznotpermanent: sure! want dance lessons?

After a quick "ha ha. NOT," I summarized my horn teacher problem, leaving out the part about the major fight with my dad. I wanted to keep that to myself.

Itznotpermanent: mr s could help. he gives private lessons

I hadn't thought of Mr. Sebastian. It never occurred to me that he gave music lessons . . . okay, it never occurred to me that he'd be good enough to help me out. A wave of embarrassment crashed over me. I'd been making the same judgments about Mr. S. as my dad had about marching band in general—that it wasn't "real music" and didn't count . . . and that the band director wouldn't be capable of teaching me a classical piece.

I thanked Punk and put the computer back to sleep. First thing tomorrow, I'd ask Mr. Sebastian about taking over my lessons until the audition. A prickle of fear nudged my heart. What if I'd been too rude to him, and he refused?

Because if he wouldn't do it, I was in serious trouble.

I spent the rest of the afternoon in my room, sorting my classical music playlists, unwilling to face my dad. *He* should apologize to *me*, I thought, and if I went downstairs it'd be like admitting defeat.

Mom came home about an hour before dinner. I crossed the hall from the bathroom, and when I turned around she was at the top of the stairs.

"Something went on here," she said, and pointed to my room.

Obediently, I went in and sat on the bed. She pulled the door closed and leaned on the frame, folding her arms. The brass name tag from the bank was still pinned to her sweater.

"Okay, what'd I miss?" she asked. "And don't say 'nothing,' because your father is sulking in the office and said that you two 'had words.' What words did you have?"

I tried to control my emotions. "Dad said that Mrs.

Rinaldi is sick, I had no lesson today, and then we got into a big fight over whether or not I take my horn seriously." I clamped my mouth shut against the tirade threatening to flood the space between us.

My mom sighed and leaned her head against the door. "Honey," she started, "you know he just wants the best for—"

I had to cut her off.

"I'm tired of hearing that he just wants the best for me. I work my butt off, and he wants me to give up!"

"Of *course* he doesn't want you to give up." Mom sighed. "He holds you—and himself—to high standards. He wants you to achieve your goals."

I snorted at that. "Give me a break. *Nothing* is ever good enough for him! And *you're* always stressed about unknown dangers," I cried, flinging Mom into the drama too. "It's ridiculous!" So much for control.

"Your father knows how talented you are, and he wants you to be successful. As for me ..." She shrugged, helpless. "I'm your mother and I worry about things. About *you*."

"So knowing I'm talented means he doesn't have to acknowledge it to me, ever? Whatever." I collapsed onto the poor pillow I'd tortured earlier. "And sometimes your worrying is just over the top," I added, voice muffled.

She nodded, surprising me. "You know what? You're right about your dad. One hundred percent. This is something that the two of you need to work out together."

I was glad that she agreed with me, but her comment was a little too similar to Jake saying that he didn't want to get in the middle of me and the Hector/Sarah disaster. What I wanted was for her to fix everything—and give me a hug. My insides felt raw, and a major part of me was still really, really hurt by what my dad had said about my commitment to the horn.

My mom crossed the room and smoothed my hair, then gave me a peck on the head and the hug I so badly needed. "I'll try to worry less, but I can't make any guarantees."

"Thanks, Mom," I muttered.

"Sometimes it's not easy to be talented and hardworking," she added before she left.

That was the understatement of the year.

32

My dad had a concert that night, so we didn't have round two of our fight over the dinner table. Instead, I ate in near-silence with my mom. Even though I was glad that my dad wasn't there, I just wanted to get my apology and focus on my audition pieces and solo. Until that happened, this situation was just one big distraction. Can't imagine where I got that phrase.

The next morning I got ready for school early so Mom could drop me off on her way to work. I wanted to talk to Mr. Sebastian first thing, instead of waiting until after practice at the end of the day. Because if he said no, I needed to find another option, fast.

Mom deposited me in the empty parking lot closest to the band room, giving me déjà vu to my first day of band camp. When I got to the door, I thought I'd arrived too early—the lights were off inside. Embarrassed and desperate, I knocked. A streak of yellow light emerged from

Mr. Sebastian's office, followed by Mr. S. He let me in.

"What a surprise, Elsie! Looking for an early-morning practice session?"

"No." I shook my head. "I wanted to talk to you, actually." I shifted from foot to foot, uncomfortable.

"Let's sit." He pointed to the risers we sat on before practice. I tucked my legs under me and clenched my necklace. "Okay, shoot," he said.

After the conversation we'd had about this a week ago, I didn't know how to ask for his help without sounding snotty. Where to start? What to say?

"You know I'm applying for Shining Birches," I began.

"I remember our discussion about it," he said dryly.

"Uh . . . yeah. Well, I kind of might need some help with that," I said.

"What do you mean?"

I picked at a spot on the industrial carpeting. "Well, I just found out that my private teacher has an emergency and can't help me, and I need to work with someone to get my audition pieces right." Mr. Sebastian didn't say anything, just watched me like he knew that I wasn't finished. "And I thought that, since you asked me to do the Sousa solo, and that's pretty stressful on top of everything else . . . I was hoping that you could maybe help me . . . figure out who could help me out with my pieces."

Mr. Sebastian raised an eyebrow. "Let me get this straight. You are asking me to help you figure out who you can work with until the Shining Birches audition; and, because I gave you a solo, this would make things even?"

Realizing how ridiculous it sounded, I nodded, miserable.

He rubbed his chin, like he was thinking hard. "Hmmm . . . I don't know if I know anyone who gives brass lessons . . ."

A pit of fear opened in my stomach. I'd blown it. He wasn't going to help me.

"It's just—I'm really stuck and stressed," I blurted.

"I was just teasing, Elsie! It's okay!" He studied my face carefully. "You are *really* worried about this."

I nodded again.

"It's just—I want to do well at my audition, and I really want to do a good job at the parade, and it just feels like everything is too much all of a sudden." I clamped my mouth shut. It had gotten *way* ahead of my brain!

Mr. Sebastian frowned. "I'm sorry that the solo for Darcy's is adding to the pressure you're feeling. I honestly wouldn't have given it to you if I knew it was going to cause you this much anxiety. But I know you can do it, Elsie. You are talented and a strong enough player to pull off both beautifully.

"And of course I will help you between now and Thanksgiving. I'll stick around and we can work in the afternoons and at lunch."

I was relieved, but the fear of not being prepared—of

blowing the whole audition—was hard to shake. After all I'd been through with my dad this fall, I *had* to get in. If I didn't, and had to wait a year, I'd basically be admitting that I wasn't cut out to be a professional musician. I only hoped that Mr. Sebastian could help me.

"Can I have your horn teacher's name? I'll get in touch with him and we'll come up with a plan. Just remember us when you get in, Elsie." His eyes twinkled.

A wave of gratitude swept through me. Just hearing that *someone* had confidence in me gave me hope that I could pull this off. Maybe, just maybe, I could do it all and make it work.

33

I thought prepping for a field show took a lot of work; working on a parade routine for a nationally televised celebration made any rehearsal before this look like a nursery school music class. Once we were done with brutal sectionals, where we played and played and played the medley until our fingers locked up, Kip and AJ marched us back and forth across the football field in our parade block, perfecting our eight to five steps and straight lines. Oh, and did I mention we did this with our instruments up, but not actually playing them?

Yeah. It was pretty awesome.

Mr. Sebastian even added an additional parade rehearsal on the Saturday morning before Thanksgiving. I spent so much time with Sousa, I could play the medley in my sleep—if I had time to sleep, that is.

All I was doing was playing one horn or the other. Luckily, the week before Thanksgiving we didn't have that much homework. I barely did any of it. My days looked something like this:

- wake up thirty minutes early, work on audition pieces with practice mute inserted
- school
- at lunch, go to the band room. Run through "Stars and Stripes Forever" solo two or three times. Use remaining time to practice audition pieces, no mute
- afternoon: parade practice Mon, Wed, Fri. Before and after each session, work on audition pieces with Mr. Sebastian
- Tues/Thurs: work with Mr. Sebastian on audition pieces
- go home, eat dinner, practice audition pieces in my room with mute in so Dad can't hear if he's home.

Rinse, repeat.

Outside of practice, I barely saw Jake. He was polite and cool, and I'd pretty much resigned myself to the fact that I'd blown it with him. Same with Hector and Sarah. I'd basically given up trying to talk with them. My heart ached for the lost friendships—and whatever Jake and I might have been—in a way that was far worse than when Alisha left. I threw myself into my horn even more.

I never saw my family, which, considering the unresolved drama between my dad and me was probably a good thing, and I had no idea how I was going to survive the weekend of craziness—or what would happen when it was over. But, on the positive side, working with Mr. Sebastian was great—much to my surprise. He knew the pieces I had to learn for the audition, and, even better than just knowing them, he'd played them! Plus, he was in touch with Mr. Rinaldi, so I felt like I actually had a chance.

Tuesday, two days before Thanksgiving, Mr. Sebastian and I were in the band room, horn at my lips, working through the audition pieces for the zillionth time. I tapped my foot to keep the beat, and as my fingers depressed the keys on my instrument, I found that place where all of a sudden it's not me who's playing—the music flows from the horn and I'm just its conduit. The melody was light, but the sound of the horn was honey-rich. Together, they created a warm dance that wove through the band room— a total "Ode to Joy" moment for me.

I finished the piece, letting the last note ring, and put the horn in my lap. My lips tingled. Mr. Sebastian applauded, and I smiled.

"Congratulations, Elsie!" he said. "That was just beautiful."

He was right. I knew it in not a bragging way, but in an "I'd listened to it too" way. I had it in me to nail this audition. I was so excited!

I just wished I had someone to share the moment with, or call after I got home.

"Thank you," I replied, and smiled again. "I couldn't have done this without your help."

Mr. Sebastian handed me the sheet music off the stand

and grabbed its base, ready to put it on the rack at the front of the room.

"You and Mr. Rinaldi did the hard work—I just came in at the end. No matter what happens, Elsie, remember this moment. You can—and will—get into that program if you play like this on Saturday."

My heart swelled with pride. As he crossed the room, something in his walk reminded me of my dad, and my heart deflated a little bit. I wished he was as proud of me as Mr. Sebastian was. He would be, I admonished myself, once I got in.

"Don't forget to bring your bags with you to school tomorrow. The bus leaves right after seventh period." Mr. Sebastian offered this last reminder as he locked the door to his office. "We'll have a long, exciting day."

I packed up my horn and returned my chair to the stacks that lined the room, thinking about how hard I'd worked for this one weekend . . . and, right after that, I realized that this weekend was all I had. Two solos. I should have been really excited for the traveling part of the trip and thrilled to go on an adventure with my friends, but all I felt was loss: two lost friends. One lost . . . whatever Jake was. Or would've been. Spending all this time practicing seemed like a good idea at the time—I was certainly prepared for what I had to do—but that's all I was. Prepared.

And I made a decision: I needed to stop playing and start fixing things. By the time I came to school on Monday, I wanted everything to be different—I'd have been on national TV, playing a solo for millions of people on an instrument that barely four months ago I'd never heard of, and I'd have auditioned for Shining Birches. And hopefully, definitely, gotten in. And hopefully gotten my friends back.

That night, after dinner, I packed my bag. As I was zipping it closed, Mom came upstairs, phone in hand.

"Grandpa wants to talk to you." She handed me the phone.

Grandpa Ozzie is my dad's dad. He lives in Florida with my grandma and still plays his horn in a couple of senior orchestras down there.

"Elsie, love!" His scratchy voice was always music to my ears. "I hear you're leaving for a big trip tomorrow."

"Yes, Grandpa—to New York, for the parade." Mom stepped into the hall, giving me privacy.

"That's turning into a regular family tradition. Did you know that I performed in the Darcy's parade too?"

"*What*? You did?!" I couldn't believe it.

"It was about forty years or so ago. I was with a contingent of the BSO. We were on a float. The biggest live audience I've ever played in front of. What a great moment for the group!" He chuckled. "Have a wonderful time. It's a special event."

"Thanks, Grandpa," I said, heart warm at his words, especially the tradition part. I had no idea that he'd ever played in a parade. And it would be a great moment for our group too, I realized. I'd been so busy thinking about it being a great moment for *me*, I'd, well, pulled an Elsie.

"And, sweetheart, good luck at the Shining Birches audition this weekend. I know you'll play well, just remember to have fun while you're in there."

I told him I loved him and we hung up. It seemed that, when it came to my horn, unlike my dad, Grandpa always knew the right thing to say to make me feel better. I whistled a little Beethoven while I packed stuff to do on the bus. Mom returned a couple of minutes later.

"Your father wanted me to say good-bye to you for him." Her forehead creased, vertical pleats appearing between her eyes.

"Uh-huh," I said, not looking at her. Dad had a matinee show and an evening performance, and hadn't come home for dinner in between. He hadn't apologized or said anything to me about the horn since our blowup, even though Mom insisted that she'd spoken to him. Well, whatever. I didn't care. I had more exciting stuff to plan for. I ignored a prickly-hot feeling and plopped my hands on top of my bag.

"I think I have everything," I said.

"He loves you, Elsie," Mom tried. She covered one of my hands with her own. "He just . . ."

"Doesn't love that I'm in marching band. I get it," I snapped. I didn't want to have this conversation tonight, not when I had so many good things to look forward to. "Whatever."

"*I'm* proud of you," Mom said. "I know I don't have a horn to toot about it, but really, Elsie, you have done so much, and grown so much since you started school. I'm impressed." Mom's heartfelt words brought me to the edge of tears. I struggled, and gave up. Wrapping my arms around her tightly, I squeezed as hard as I could.

"I'm glad you don't have any horns to toot," I whispered to her.

She finished the hug and went back downstairs, leaving me to a night of crazy dreams and half sleep.

Miraculously, Dad made an appearance before I left for school. When he plays a double show he gets home late and typically sleeps in until eight or nine. I dropped my duffel bag on the floor and rummaged through the fridge. An apple and a slice of chocolate chip muffin bread looked appealing. I purposely focused on my food—taking time to wash the apple and carefully unwrapping the bread—so I didn't have to talk with him. He should say something first.

"Today's the big day," he began. I settled my slice of bread on a ragged sheet of paper towel.

"Well, tomorrow is," I replied. "Today's a travel day." From watching him through my whole childhood, I knew the right terms to use.

"Look, Elsie, about what went on last week . . . I'm sorry. I know that marching band has become important to you, and I'm glad that you've found a musical niche at school."

"Found a musical niche?" Offended, I stuffed a chunk of muffin bread into my mouth to prevent myself from saying anything that would get me in trouble.

He shifted and sighed. Wearing his blue plaid robe, hair a little mussed and eyes groggy behind his glasses, he looked vulnerable, like he'd expected to say something wrong. He wasn't a hundred percent awake.

"I'm just glad you're happy in marching band, Elsie. And I know you'll perform beautifully at the parade and audition. Your group really impressed me at the competition a few weeks ago, and I'm sorry I didn't get to tell you that." His expression was guarded, like he was so sure I was going to be mad or say something awful to him, I immediately felt bad.

"Thanks, Dad," I said, and gave him a hug.

If that was his apology, why did I still feel so hollow?

34

School dragged by slower than a mouse towing a concrete block across a football field. Like everyone else, I'd stashed my duffel bag in the band room before first period. During morning announcements, the crackly voice over the PA blared congratulations and wished us good luck in New York. A few kids in my homeroom even cheered.

This was a big deal. A very big deal. I'd be playing a solo on TV, alone.

When seventh period finally ended, I crammed all of my books into my locker—why bother pretending, no work was getting done this weekend!—and raced to the band room. Seniors and juniors with no seventh period were already there, and the space was a jumbled, chaotic hub of activity. I flashed back to the first day of band camp, when I didn't understand anything that was going on. Now I knew exactly what was happening: instruments getting packed, uniforms loaded, luggage hauled out to the big charter buses . . . and I was part of it. Or, at least, I was partially part of it. As I watched the other band members laughing and joking with one another, I missed my friends. I wanted Hector to ask me another goofy classical music question, or for Sarah to show me the latest jewelry trends . . . or Jake to hold my hand. I wanted to have the time to get to know more about them. I needed to apologize. To try and make things right one last time.

When all of the buses and the truck were loaded, AJ and Mr. Sebastian called us together.

"We're just about ready," called AJ, "and we'll be boarding the buses in ten minutes. Before we do, there are a couple of logistical things that we need to go over."

Mr. Sebastian pulled a sheet of paper from his pocket. "This is the trip schedule." He shook it for emphasis. "One thing I didn't tell you earlier is that we'll be doing a recording session prior to step-off. All parade performances are taped in advance in case of a weather problem or emergency. We are slated to record at two forty-five a.m."

My jaw—along with everyone else's—fell open. *What?!*

Mr. Sebastian went on before anyone could say anything. "This is how it's done. There are over two hundred performances that happen during the parade, and all of them need to be taped and edited before step-off. We are given a fifteen-minute window. After which, we'll have a very early breakfast, you'll snooze on the bus, then we'll get into uniform and be at our step-off location at six thirty."

He went on, giving details about how we'd get our instruments and what would happen to the buses while we performed, but I didn't bother to listen. The idea of being up basically all night and marching the next day was both terrifying and thrilling. I tried not to think about how tired I'd be on the ride home. I could sleep the whole time, practice all day Friday, and be totally recharged and ready for my audition on Saturday. Right?

Mr. Sebastian finally finished talking and we loaded onto the buses. I was one of the last ones on; I waited, since I essentially had no one to sit with. Sarah, Jake, and Hector grabbed seats toward the back, with Steve and Punk. Punk gave me a shy smile and I smiled back as I climbed the stairs. I guess it was kind of cool that he thought of a less-pierced version of himself when he saw me, but I wished his good intentions hadn't helped me mess things up with Jake. As I balanced in the aisle, trying to figure out where to sit on the totally full bus, the driver called out in a gravelly voice, "Please take your seat! If you're standing, you are a hazard and a projectile!"

I blushed and everyone around me cracked up.

"The chicken is a projectile!" someone yelled. "Incoming!" That brought another round of laughter. I clutched the seats and wanted to die.

Jake caught my eye and gestured to the empty seat next to him. He wanted me to sit with him? I tried to rein in the elation that coursed through me and reminded myself to focus.

"Thanks," I squeaked, and plopped into the seat. Suddenly I didn't have any more words to say. Luckily, some action in the aisle saved me. Steve and Punk were huddled together, up to no good, I was sure. Finished with their nefarious schemes, they slid into the seat across the back of the bus.

Steve got up to talk to AJ. "Don't go back there," he whispered on his way to his seat, and winked.

Yikes! What were they up to?

Jake, meanwhile, was fiddling with the zipper on his backpack. Now or never, Elsie, I told myself.

"I'm really sorry," I said. Saying it was easier because his head was down. "And I know you're mad at me, and that I've messed up . . . everything, but I just want you to know that I like you and I'm sorry and this trip will stink if I have no friends to share it with." I was breathless and tears were coming. I really, really didn't want to cry.

I could feel Sarah and Hector staring at me from across the aisle. I hoped that Jake would move, or look at me, or say something. My heart pounded in my chest.

He tucked his backpack under the bus seat and leaned back.

"You make it tough for people to like you, Elsie," he said.

"I know." I hung my head. "I'm an awful, no-good, very bad friend. Seriously."

"I don't know if you're *that* bad," Jake responded. Was he teasing me?

"I'm trying to be better, but I don't know if I can *get* better if I have no friends to practice on." At this point, I could see Hector and Sarah out of the corner of my eye, obviously listening to me, so I turned directly to them. Both were staring at me, dead on.

"Look," I said, trying to continue with my apology, "I know I'm a freak, okay? And I want to change. I'm *trying* to change."

Sarah and Hector exchanged glances. Next to me, Jake sighed.

"Can you?" Jake said. "Change can be good, but, Elsie, you've really hurt us."

"I want us to hang out again. I didn't mean to get you guys so mad at me. It's just . . . it's hard for me to be close with anyone or thing—other than my horn. And that doesn't have feelings." Weird as it sounded, it was the truth. And, thankfully, Hector, Sarah, and Jake seemed to realize that.

"You need to use your mouth less, brain more," Hector said. "Especially when it comes to me."

I nodded at him.

"One more example of jerky, insensitive behavior and I'm done," growled Sarah. "Seriously."

"I know. I'm so sorry." I was so grateful that they were listening to me, that things between us could maybe get better if I changed.

Jake reached out and squeezed my hand, and I knew that he understood that I didn't mean for things with Punk to get so weird. The whole time, I felt . . . what was the word? Remorseful. Like if I could go back and change everything, I would. This time I *really* needed to learn and change. No more second chances.

As I was thinking about that, Sarah popped up.

"Oh! I can't find my cell phone!" She made a show of patting her pockets while Hector searched their seat. As she reached up to the overhead bin to grab her bag, I saw it peeking out of her pocket. Before opening my mouth to tell her, though, I noticed that her eyes kept dancing toward the back of the bus—and Steve.

Oh! *OH!* That's what she wanted me to ask her about after the Halloween dance! I was such a dolt. Realizing that Sarah was crushing on Steve and trying to get his attention nearly made me laugh out loud. I clamped my lips closed, vowing to ask her about him when we got to New York.

Jake sat in the seat next to me, closest to the window. He took my hand. My heart pounded and palms dampened, and it was easy to put Sarah and Steve out of my mind.

"This is going to be so awesome," he said. I smiled and tried to calm down. Having him next to me was like sitting next to a low-level electrical charge: The hair on my arms would stand up every so often, and a scatter of sparks zapped across the back of my neck when I looked at him. How did *I* get so lucky?

"New York City, here we come!" called Jake.

"Whooo!!" everyone responded. "Goooo Hellcats!"

AJ made his way to the middle of the bus, arms draped over seats on either side for balance. "Let me hear you!" he called. "One-two-three-four!"

"Screaming Hellcats at the door!" we responded. It was one of our pre-performance psych-up chants.

"Five-six-seven-eight!" he yelled.

"Blowin' you out of our way!" we cheered. "*Gooo*, Hellcats!" Screams and yells reverberated off the bus ceiling. Jake and I exchanged giant smiles. Inside, as I listened to the cheers ricocheting up and down the aisle, I was filled to nearly bursting with happiness. I *belonged* here. I hadn't felt that way about anything else. Yeah, I was always comfortable when I was playing or sitting in an orchestra, but, maybe because of my dad, I'd looked at playing in those ensembles as *jobs*. I'd focused on learning my parts and playing well, and hadn't really connected with anyone—as Sarah kept pointing out. Now, as I looked at Sarah's, Jake's, and Hector's beaming faces, Steve's lazy smile, and Punk's loopy grin, something clicked. I could do what I loved—play my instrument—have friends, and feel like I was part of something larger than myself. And it felt *good*. I squeezed Jake's hand, wrapped around mine, and smiled at him.

Everything was going to be okay.

35

A little while later, Jake took out a deck of cards from his bag. I'm not a card player, but he and Sarah and Hector taught me how to play a game called Pig. We played for a while, then I needed to go to the bathroom. We'd been on the road for a little over an hour, but the only scheduled rest stop was another forty minutes away. I definitely couldn't wait that long.

I bowed out of the game and slipped out of my seat. Across the back, Steve and Punk were watching a movie on a laptop, earbuds in and eyes riveted to the screen. Hadn't Steve said something about not coming back here? I thought as I folded the tiny bathroom door closed behind me. Maybe they're watching something they're not supposed to.

When I finished washing my hands, I grabbed the ring that passed for a knob and it came off in my grasp. A square black hole appeared where the knob should have been.

Fighting a wave of panic, I tried to fit the knob-piece back into the hole. It wouldn't stay. Then I stuck my finger in the hole and rattled the door, trying to get it to budge. No dice. Whatever mechanism locked it was stuck.

I was trapped in the bus bathroom on the highway in the middle of Connecticut. I pounded on the door.

"Guys!! Guys!" I called. "Lemme out!" I waited. Nothing. Punk and Steve were plugged in and tuned out, so I knew they wouldn't hear me. The seat up against the bathroom was filled with coats and a few pieces of luggage, no help there. I shook the door again, and yelled as loud as I could, over and over again.

"I! Am! Stuck!"

Finally, Punk's voice came through the tiny hole where the knob used to live.

"Who's in there?"

"Me! Elsie."

"Elsie?! Crud." Punk's voice grew a little fainter as he moved away from the door. "Steve! Elsie's locked in the bathroom."

Steve uttered some pretty creative swears. "I told you not to go in there!" he said.

"*You* did this?!" I screeched. Of course. That's what they'd been up to—they'd been messing with the knob when we came on the bus. "Fix it and get me out!"

"Okay, okay. Hold your horses," came Steve's voice.

"I am stuck in a *bathroom*!" I shrieked. "I am *not* holding my horses."

"Elsie? Elsie? Calm down." Jake's voice joined the boys'. "Just calm down. We'll get you out." I tried to regain control of myself, so he wouldn't think I was a total lunatic, but I was so embarrassed, I wanted to die.

"Elsie," came Steve's fake-happy voice, "we've, uh, encountered a little problem."

"Uh-huh . . ." I said through gritted teeth. "Littler than me being stuck in the bathroom? Because this is a pretty *big* problem, as far as I can tell, Steve."

I imagined Steve, Jake, and Punk exchanging glances. Oh, who was I kidding? Everyone knew what was going on by now. My face flamed. Zombie Chicken was going to sound like the best nickname ever once they coined ones from this disaster.

"We—*ow!*—okay, *I* broke a screw." Punk sounded apologetic. "I, uh, think we're going to have to call for help. Stay right there."

"Where the *heck* am I going to go?" And what did "call for help" mean? 911? The state police? Were they going to have to use the Jaws of Life to get me out? I'd be on the news, and my mother's wacky newsmagazine fears would have come true.

"Who are you calling?" I said.

"They went to get Mr. Sebastian," Hector responded, confirming my suspicions about being the Spectacle of the Trip.

A second later, Mr. Sebastian chimed in.

"Elsie, are you all right?" His concerned tone nearly brought me to tears. I'd been trapped for over twenty minutes.

"Yuh-yes," I stuttered. I regained some control. "I'm okay."

"Listen, we're going to stop at a rest area in about ten minutes and we're going to get you out. Just hang in there. And *you* two"—I assumed this was directed at Punk and Steve—"you two are in for it. *Big*-time."

I leaned against the carpet-covered wall of my antiseptic-smelling prison and caught my reflection in the mirror. My cheeks were red and blotchy, and my hair was a disaster. I tried to pull myself together for the impending rescue, and found that, despite being completely annoyed at Steve and Punk, I saw a glimmer of humor at the whole situation. Not that I'd let anyone think I found this funny.

Jake, Hector, Sarah, Steve, Punk, and Mr. Sebastian chatted with me through the door until we arrived at the rest area. The bus slowed down, then hit speed bumps pulling into the parking lot. The sink dug into my side. We slowed to a stop, but my heart sped up. How would they get me out?

"They're letting everyone off the bus for a, err, bathroom break," Jake said through the door. "I don't think anyone wants to use this one."

"I don't blame them," I said dryly.

"Elsie," Mr. Sebastian said. "We're going to take a new approach. Do you see the window?"

I glanced at the tiny window way above the toilet. Oh, man. Were they thinking . . .

"It's an emergency exit." A gruff, gravelly voice—the bus driver's, most likely—joined the conversation. "There's a rubber piece that pulls off around the frame, and you pop the window out. Do you see?"

I saw. A little tag that read "pull in case of emergency" was posted at the base of the window. "You want me to *climb out the window?*" I asked, incredulous. "SERIOUSLY?"

"I'm afraid we have no choice," Mr. Sebastian said. "Unless you want to ride the rest of the way to New York in there."

Negatory.

"Give us a minute to get outside, and we'll get ready for you. Jake will watch us and tell you when to pop the tab. Okay?"

How was this my life?

"It's not like I have any other options," I answered.

"You're doing great," Jake said through the door. "I'm totally impressed." Warmth flooded through me at his words, and, in spite of the situation, I smiled.

"Okay, I think they're ready for you," he said.

I should've spent more time looking at the layout of

the bathroom. To knock the window out, I'd have to straddle the lidless toilet seat, then hoist myself up and through the opening. Great.

I stepped onto the slick plastic, bracing myself with one hand against the wall. The neon-blue puddle inside the toilet would leave an unmistakable stain on my white sneakers if I took one wrong step. Before pulling the rubber tab, I glanced out the window.

The entire band was standing there, staring up at me. *Way* up at me.

I'd forgotten that between the luggage bays and big wheels, the charter was extra-tall. The drop looked to be about nine hundred feet—but was probably more like ten.

And Mr. Sebastian stood waiting, arms up to catch me.

36

As soon as the group saw me peek out the window, the chanting began.

"Jump! Jump! Jump!"

I was going to fall straight into Mr. Sebastian's waiting arms. Horror, embarrassment, and deadly anger combined inside of me for an emotional cocktail. My hands shook as I pulled the emergency exit seal from around the window. "Push glass to exit," read the little sign. I pushed, and the rectangular pane popped out and clattered to the pavement below. A big crack bisected the window. The band cheered.

"Okay, Elsie," Mr. Sebastian called. AJ joined him, so now I had two rescuers. "Just reach out for my arms and we'll catch you."

"Oh, man," I muttered. Could I even *fit* through a window that small? I wasn't sure I could squeeze my shoulders through. It looked about as big as a postage stamp. Trying to keep my footing on the toilet, I stood on tiptoes and stuck my arms through the window opening. My chest pressed against the frame. I leaned forward as far as I could, bent my elbows, gripped each side of the opening, and heaved.

My bandmates fell silent.

Mr. Sebastian and AJ stepped forward.

My upper body slid through with no problem, and I found myself in this weird position half in, half out of the bathroom: feet dangling above the toilet, arms braced against the outside of the bus, like a crazy figurehead on a ship.

"C'mon, Chicken! Let go! Reach for us!" AJ said. They were just below me. AJ could have stood on his toes and grabbed my wrists. "We'll pull you out!"

Mouth dry, I did what he said. I bent at the waist, toward the ground, so I wouldn't fall back into the bathroom. The window ledge cut into my body at my belly button. I had to hang my head down, so all I could see was the dirty gray side of the bus. My heart beat louder than a bass drum. All of this happened in the split second it took AJ to grab my surprisingly freezing and dry palms in his warm hands. He tugged, my stomach scraped against the window frame, and I fell—right into a pair of arms that grabbed me awkwardly at the waist. A cheer went up from the crowd and Mr. Sebastian put me down gently. My knees shook and I fought the urge to hide.

"The chicken flies!" yelled AJ triumphantly. He raised

my hands—which he hadn't let go of—over my head in a victory salute. They all expected me to freak out, to turn chicken and run.

Not today.

"Buck-buck ba-gawk!" I squawked as loud as I could, finally getting it. I was Chicken because I belonged, not because I *didn't* fit in.

"Yeaaahhh!!" everyone yelled. Mr. Sebastian cracked up. Hector, Sarah, and Jake appeared at my elbow for hugs and high fives. I thanked Mr. Sebastian and AJ, and looked at the crowd that remained.

"Anyone need to pee?" I called. "Bathroom's free!"

37

Luckily, the rest of the ride to New York was nowhere near as interesting or entertaining. Happy to be sitting in a seat instead of locked in a germy cubicle, I played a few more hands of Pig with Hector, Sarah, and Jake, and then rested my head on Jake's shoulder to take a nap. Feeling his heat through his shirt, I didn't think I'd be able to sleep, but I guess being locked in a bathroom takes a lot out of a person, because soon I was asleep.

We arrived in Manhattan a little before seven, just in time for dinner. The buses took us to a big chain restaurant, where we ate fast and got right back on for our ride to the hotel. Since we received our invitation so late, and there were so many people in town for the parade, most of the hotels in the city were booked. We had to stay in New Jersey—although "stay" was putting it lightly. We arrived at nearly ten, and had a one a.m. wake-up call so we could shower and ride back into Manhattan for our middle of the night recording session. Basically, it'd be a glorified nap.

Sarah and I shared a room with two freshmen woodwind players, who thought the jokes they made when I went into the bathroom to brush my teeth were hysterical.

At one point I nudged Sarah. "Thanks for finally accepting my apology," I said, shy. "I missed hanging out with you."

"And I missed your clueless and annoying comments," she said. But she was smiling when she spoke, and I knew she was kidding.

"Anything you want to tell me?" I asked, changing the subject.

She stared at me blankly.

"Anything . . . about my section leader?" I gave her a mischievous grin.

Her face lit up. "*Finally*, Elsie!"

She talked my ear off for an hour about him, until finally the other girls convinced us to watch a cheesy romantic comedy to kill time. I dozed a little, but we were all awake when the phone rang at one. Forty minutes later, we were back on the bus.

"Did you sleep at all?" I asked Jake. This time, I was in the window seat. Neon dotted the darkness. Jake shook his head.

"No way." He'd shared a room with Hector and two trumpet players. "Steve, Punk, AJ, and Mac were next door to us. Our rooms were connected, so we hung out and played cards." He yawned. "I beat them at hearts four times, and made them swear they'd never lock you in a bathroom again."

I grinned. "Thanks. You are too thoughtful."

"And I'll be keeping you close by," he said. He snuggled lower in his seat and regarded me with his big hazel eyes. My heart pounded, and my palms became slick.

"Uh, how close?" I squeaked.

"Close," he said. He leaned in—close. Closer. Closest . . .

His lips touched mine, and a fizzy, buzzy shock burst through my body. I was so surprised, I sat straight up and broke the kiss. Cool, Elsie. Cool.

He looked hurt. "Are you okay?"

"Yuh-yeah," I stammered. "Fine. I just . . . it just . . . it was nice," I finished lamely.

"Nice," he said.

I nodded. "Very."

"Nice enough to try that again?"

I pretended to consider his answer while I tried to regain control of my staccato beating heart.

"I suppose," I said. I scooched down in the seat, leaned toward him, and closed my eyes. This time, I was somewhat prepared for the delicious jolty feeling, and I didn't freak out. I just did my best to kiss him back. He pulled away, breaking the kiss, and I opened my eyes.

"That okay?" I asked, shy. He slipped his arm through mine.

"I'd say so," he said.

"Jake," I said, unsure, "can I ask you a question?" He nodded, and I went on. "It's just . . . I don't know why you like me. I mean, I'm glad that you do—you are one of the nicest, most considerate people I know—and I'm so . . . prickly."

"You forgot good-looking," he teased. "I'm nice, considerate, and good-looking." I swatted at him and he grabbed my hands. "Seriously, Elsie? You don't know?"

I shook my head, suddenly feeling all teary and not knowing why.

"You're just . . . you're different. You work harder than anyone I know. You love music. You say what you mean— sometimes that can get you in trouble, but you don't want to hurt people on purpose. And you have a great smile, for a chicken."

His words warmed me. I didn't know what to say back, so I settled for giving him the biggest hug I could. He kissed me on the head, a quick peck. "I think we should try and get some rest before the dress rehearsal," he said, and yawned again.

I tilted my head onto his shoulder. The bus tires hummed, the engine growled, and Jake's rhythmic breathing filled my mind as I drifted off.

The next thing I knew, Jake was shaking me and the bus had stopped.

"Time to get into uniform!" Sarah popped over the seat in front of us.

Jake squeezed my hand and slid out. "Hope it was a good nap," he said.

I nodded. Sarah tugged on my arm. "Let's *go*!" she squealed. "This is so *exciting*!"

Her enthusiasm was contagious, and I was grateful to share it with her. I let her propel me down the bus aisle and into the street. The night air was cold and crisp. Around us, the stores and restaurants were shuttered and dark, their neon signs black and skeletal against the windows. The equipment truck was parked a little ways down the block.

Sarah and I walked toward it, rubbing our shoulders, breath fogging. When we grabbed our uniform bags, the band parents handing them out told us that we'd have to get in line for warm-ups in ten minutes.

We raced to get dressed, and I left Sarah to get my mellophone out from under the bus. Above the luggage bay, the dark bathroom window gaped, a reminder of what happened earlier that day. It *felt* like it had happened in another lifetime. Sleeping in those weird bursts and being outside so late at night had my internal clock all messed up; I had no idea what time it was or whether or not I was supposed to be asleep or awake.

I found my mellophone case and put my instrument

together, snapping the clasps and shoving the empty box under the belly of the bus just as AJ started shouting for everyone to set up. Quickly, I scurried through the lines to my spot between Punk and Steve.

"You two are *so* dead," I growled at them.

"Dude, Elsie, you weren't supposed to go in there!" Punk whispered at me through gritted teeth. "We *told* you!"

"I have major plans for the two of you," I rumbled. The expressions on their faces were hilarious. Wait 'til they see what's up my sleeve, I thought.

AJ called us to attention.

"We're going to run through fifteen minutes of warm-ups," he began, "then we're going to march to the parade review area. There are residences all around, so I expect that you will play softly while we're here, and when we march over we'll be using a one-snare tap to keep time. The review area is lit for filming. We'll march in to our regular cadence, perform our parade pieces, and march out. Got that?"

Not that we could answer or anything.

All through warm-ups, it felt as if an entire marching band was doing drill in my stomach. I was nervous, excited, terrified—anything and everything you could imagine. Plus, I was still thinking about that kiss (okay, *those kisses*) with Jake. There was so much emotion messing with my heart and brain, I had to concentrate extra-hard to play my instrument.

AJ cut us off, gave us an "instruments down" command, and counted off the drums so we could march to the taping area. The cracks of the snare echoed off the dark buildings in sharp snaps. It was eerie, marching along in total silence with such a big group of people in a huge city in the middle of the night. I expected something from a movie to come get us—a giant, man-eating reptile, or a ball of flame to shoot from the sky—it was so surreal.

What was even *more* surreal? Turning around a corner and seeing an entire city block lit up like it was high noon, packed with people and TV cameras. If it hadn't been for the hours and hours of marching and drill instruction I'd been subjected to since August, I would have stopped dead in my tracks, wrecking our parade block and everyone's good mood. Instead, my legs carried me forward automatically while I peered at the scene from under the brim of my shako.

Giant banks of lights stood on spidery legs attached to portable generators. They were so powerful that the shadows cast on the street were extra-sharp, as though someone went over them with a black permanent marker. Thick orange electrical cables held down with patches of duct tape snaked all over the street. Two cameras hung off mini-cranes—were they called booms?—and people scurried in a zillion different directions in the shadows behind the lights.

"Whoa," I heard Steve mutter. "This is the big time."
My thoughts exactly.

AJ stopped us just short of a huge section of the street
that had been painted blue and gold and detailed with the
Darcy's sunshine logo and "The Eighty-fifth Annual Darcy's Department Store Thanksgiving Day Parade" across
it. From years of watching the parade on TV, I knew we
were in front of the big Darcy's store, but a set of portable
bleachers blocked the main entrance. The review stand, I
guessed.

Even though I was sure they'd probably been checked
a hundred times for stability, my stomach quavered when
I saw those risers.

AJ called us to attention. A guy wearing a headset and
carrying a giant clipboard came over to him. He spoke so
loud, it was easy to hear him.

"Okay, Hellcats. On my mark, you'll begin your parade
feature, march into the performance space, play your piece,
and then march straight out to your cadence. Do not stop
playing your cadence until you reach the corner of Lexing-
ton. Got it?"

AJ nodded curtly. I took a deep breath. Was he as nervous as I was right now? He didn't look it. In his uniform,
jaw set, AJ looked—well, pretty amazing.

"Instruments *up!*" AJ called. We were ready.

Headset man stepped away and AJ shook his arms
out, eyes never leaving the guy's face. Mine didn't either.

Headset brought a hand to his ear, tilted his head in a quick jerk, and pointed straight at AJ.

We were on.

"One! Two! One-and-two-and—" We stepped off and came in.

Like it had during the fateful field show competition weeks earlier, the band just clicked. The feeling was absolutely electric, but we were in control. The Sousa marches sounded light and fun—exactly the way they were supposed to—each note separate and distinct. Kip had taught us a fancy move for when we hit the center of the performance area—the kids in the outer perimeter of the block would march clockwise, while the kids two rows in would march counterclockwise. Basically, I'd stay still while Steve and Punk marched. The color guard spun their flags inches from our heads and danced a two-step. Everyone else marked time, marching in place.

During my "Stars and Stripes" solo, I found my playing zone. My fingers danced over the valves, and the notes were light enough to leap across a stream on pinheads.

The song ended and the cadence began. AJ marched us out of the performance area and down the block. I risked sneaking glances at Punk and Steve. Both were in perfect parade formation: eyes forward, back straight, faces set and determined. But I sensed the joy coming off them.

When we finally got to the "clear zone," AJ stopped us

and put us at ease. Immediately, a roar rose from the band. We'd done it!

"That was amazing!" AJ shouted over us. "Ab-so-flapping-*lutely* amazing!"

We screamed and jumped up and down, everyone hugging one another and cheering, until, from above us came a shout.

"Knock it off! I'm sleepin' here! It's three a.m.!"

"I can't believe we just did that," Sarah squealed. She came from the front of the block, flag flapping, to find me. "And you sounded incredible!" She hugged me.

Jake and Hector appeared from behind her, hats hanging from their arms by the chin straps and uniforms partially unbuttoned, smiling crooked smiles.

"Awesome. Just awesome," Jake said. Hector slapped high fives.

I was so pumped, I'd never need to sleep again. And this wasn't even the real thing.

38

AJ, Mr. Sebastian, and the band parents corralled us and ushered us back to the buses so we could change and have breakfast. At four a.m. On Thanksgiving.

I didn't care. I'd never felt this good about any performance I'd done: field show, orchestral, or otherwise. I was flying higher than the Empire State Building, reliving every moment with my friends as we ate pancakes and French toast . . . and as I swigged most of Jake's coffee. Banned substance in my house or not, I knew I'd need the caffeine to get through the morning.

Everyone'd said the same thing over and over again: "And that's with no people out there! This is going to be crazy!!" And every single person had something nice to say about my solo, which was awesome. It wiped Shining Birches from my mind—for the time being.

What felt like minutes later, I was changing back into my uniform next to Sarah and preparing for warm-ups as streaks of sunlight bled across the night sky. Exhaustion crept in. I could see it on everyone's faces—and I'm sure mine looked the same way: dark circles, skin slightly paler than usual, eyes a touch red.

We were back on the bus, weaving through blocked-off streets to the spot near Central Park where we'd line up. The parade began at nine, but we had to be in our spot by six thirty so they could clear the buses out and fully close the streets. I nudged Jake and pointed at the people huddled under blankets and sitting on folding chairs along the route. They'd already staked out parade spots!

"Pretty awesome," he said. I agreed.

The bus stopped.

"Everyone off!" AJ yelled.

We spent the next few hours huddled in groups, chatting and keeping ourselves—and our instruments—warm by standing over the subway grates, which would occasionally let out a blast of hot air. The way that the performers were staged for step-off, we couldn't see any floats or balloons—just the other high school marching bands in front and behind us. Supposedly, though, rock star Theo Christmas would be on the Toasty Oats Cereal "Holidaze in the Jungle" float in front of our band. Sadly, we'd never see him, though—balloons and floats entered the parade via a different street.

By eight, both the early-morning post-performance high and the "check out that other band" competitiveness had worn off, and all that was keeping me going were caffeine-infused jitters from Jake's coffee. When AJ told us to form our block, I was grateful that the day was almost over—and it hadn't started yet!

We lined up and the band parents swept through, offering sips from water bottles and a final lint brush swipe. AJ counted off, and the cadence began, a little sluggish at first. We marched down the block, past the groups that were farther back in the parade than us, and then, when we turned a corner, I saw:

The canyon of buildings rising up from the street.

The people stacked at least ten deep on the sidewalk.

The viewers hanging out on fire escapes and balconies.

The ginormous SpongeBob balloon floating a block in front of us.

Adrenaline electrified me. This was the biggest, coolest, most amazing moment in my life—and I realized that very few would ever beat it. And it was because of marching band.

Luckily, my marching brain was still paying attention, because suddenly I found myself playing. I'd barely been aware of AJ's command, but my body had responded automatically. We had a three-song program: the HeHe High fight song, a Christmas tune (after all, the parade officially kicked off the holiday shopping season), and the Sousa medley. AJ created simple hand signals to delineate which one we were supposed to play at any given time, which was good, because the roar of the crowd made it nearly impossible to hear him.

We marched at a slow pace and had to stop at every half block as groups farther up the line performed at the review stand. I didn't mind. It gave me the opportunity to try and capture the experience, burn it into my brain.

About thirty blocks of marching later, we approached the performance area. AJ cut us off, giving our chops a break from the near-constant playing. My lips and cheeks buzzed, and I needed to gear up to tackle that solo again. During the night—morning?—a camera guy had been right in my face, and when we were live everyone would know it was me playing that solo. My mom and dad would see *me*. On TV. I swelled with pride and excitement.

"It's go time!" shouted AJ. I could barely hear him over the crowd.

He gave the signal and the snares snapped: *Crack! Crack! Crack-crack-crack!*

We stepped off.

39

The review stand was packed tighter than a whale in a bikini. The band marched into the performance field, Sousa medley sounding just as good as it had at our three a.m. rehearsal. I played conservatively to be safe, reining in so I could let loose during the big solo, but my cheeks and lips ached from the long day.

The rotating boxes began. Punk and Steve stepped off, leaving me alone, marking time. A flag spun perilously close to my head as a color guard member stumbled, but I didn't even flinch. The roar of the crowd faded into a low buzz as I honed in on the music. Our sound enveloped me just as it had on the first day of band camp, awing me with its power and beauty. Swiftly, I stripped off my gloves and stuck them in my sleeve—I'd found it easier to play the solo without them.

Right before the solo, the entire band turned to face the crowd. I was ready: lost in the pride and intensity of the march, the high from the crowd, the amazingness of the whole experience. All the parts of our performance— the music, the solo, marching, Sarah and the color guard's flag work—meshed together in a complex arrangement that created art and music in a way no orchestra ever could.

And right then, like the largest lightbulb in Times Square had turned on in my brain, I finally understood what marching band was all about: the band. It was bigger and cooler than anything I could ever do alone.

Even though the majority of the band wasn't half as serious as I was about music, what we achieved as a group brought all of us much further than our individual accomplishments. Even though I wanted to play my best for *me*, I also wanted to play my best for them. No one would remember who I was after the solo, but they might remember the band. The Hellcats, with their weird traditions and mayhem, accepted me for who I was *as well as* what I could bring to them. The revelation nearly knocked me back on my heels.

And, following right behind that one, was a second: I didn't just like marching band.

I loved it.

And there had to be room in my life for it, even on my journey to becoming a professional horn player.

All of these thoughts ricocheted around in my head in a matter of seconds, filling me with music and joy. I took a breath, and came in on cue for the "Stars and Stripes" solo.

It sounded awesome. I rocked those notes like I'd been born to play them, pouring excitement and joy and new understanding into each one. Out of the corner of my eye, I spotted the cameraman heading my way.

Yeah!

The camera came closer. I closed my eyes to really power through those last few bars. I had to make them count.

I blocked out the crowd noise, focusing on the mellophone's sound and on the solo, hoping the cameraman was getting this. Adrenaline coursed through my veins on top of the caffeine, making me feel both sharp and trembly. My hands started to sweat.

Time to open my eyes and give a half smile to the millions of TV viewers from behind my mouthpiece when I was finished. Almost done!

The camera was about a foot away from my face, so I focused on the crowd behind it. My eyes settled on a man sitting nearly dead center in the bleachers. He wore a funky black hat—a fedora?—and round glasses like my dad's that were perched on an enormous red nose. It was amazing I could pick anyone out of the group, but my heightened, caffeinated senses were on overdrive. Something about him was vaguely—

Then I knew.

It was Richard Dinglesby, director of Shining Birches music camp. What was *he* doing here?!

Deet-deet, deet-deet, deedle-deedle-leet-deet, bleedle . . . bleedle—black-blee!

My head went fuzzy; all of the blood in it drained to my feet. A pit of horror opened in my middle. The last notes came out inarticulate, smooshed and sloppy, more like muddy puddles than the light, dancing droplets they were supposed to be.

Forget the awesomeness of my band revelations.

I gakked the solo.

On national television.

In front of Richard Dinglesby from Shining Birches.

40

I don't remember much after the disastrous end to the solo. I know I marched out of the review area with the rest of the band, I know we crossed the finish line and marched to where our buses were parked; I just have no recollection of anything except pulsing heat in my face and the weight of shame on my shoulders. I kept my eyes focused on the trumpet player's hat in front of me. I couldn't look at anyone.

I made a massive, massive mistake.

On national television.

I couldn't uphold my end of the bargain—we all worked so hard to create this moment, and I blew it.

The entire band probably hated me.

I hated myself.

Was it the caffeine? My slick hands? The shock of Richard Dinglesby sitting in the audience? I'd played the solo perfectly a bunch of times before—and had done an amazing job on it at nearly three a.m., when there was no one around to hear it!—why couldn't I do it right this time?!

My dad's voice, suggesting that I not take the solo, echoed around my brain. He was right. I took on too much. I embarrassed the Hellcats and myself, and for what? I cracked under the pressure. What did that mean for my chances at the Shining Birches audition? I didn't even want to think about that.

The buses were in sight. AJ stopped the group and put us at parade rest, then shouted some stuff that I didn't pay attention to and dismissed us. The whole band cheered. I clutched my horn to my chest, waiting for the anger that was sure to come my way when the yelling died down.

Instead, arms wrapped around me from behind and lifted me off the ground in a bear hug.

"Whooo! Chick-*EN*! You did it!" Steve put me down and Punk popped into my line of sight, hand raised in a high five. Red-faced and grinning, they both looked so happy they could explode.

Was this a joke?

"Don't leave me hanging!" Punk said. "C'mon!" He raised his arm a little higher.

I burst into tears.

"Chicken!" Steve said. Punk's mouth dropped into an O of surprise. "What's wrong?"

I could barely get words out.

"I guh-guh-gakked it," I said between sniffs. Jake, Hector, and Sarah had appeared, also glowing.

Punk and Steve shot glances at each other. "It was four notes, Elsie. You were *amazing* for the rest of it."

I didn't understand how they could think that. I ruined it!

"Your performance was awesome," Jake said. "Our performance was awesome. We did an amazing job!"

"Cut yourself some slack, Elsie," Hector added. "You only got the solo two weeks ago. It's totally cool."

Sarah nodded, a playful smirk on her lips. "Everyone has bad articulation sometimes," she pointed out.

I managed to crack a smile at her words.

"Don't let four notes ruin your whole experience," Steve said. "Seriously. It was *four notes*. I know that you're bummed, but let's not lose sight of the crazy fun we just had. Your bad mood is bringing me down."

"We've been playing since three a.m.," Punk reminded me. "Your chops must be shot."

Even though I wasn't one hundred percent sure that I believed all of their words, my fog of embarrassment started to lift. I didn't want to bring them down. The day *had* been pretty amazing up until those four notes . . .

"YEAH!" AJ came by, slapping fives. "Good work, Chicken," he said.

I flushed. "It didn't come out right," I said. "I'm sorry."

"Don't apologize!" he said. "Shake it off. It's done.

We just marched in the Darcy's parade!!" He kept going, offering congratulations to everyone.

I stepped back from our little group, watching how happy and excited they were about what we'd just done.

Wait . . . we HAD just done something really cool and amazing. As a group. All of us.

I'd marched through Manhattan in the biggest parade in the country, if not the world, playing my instrument.

I'd performed a solo on national television.

I'd done it with my friends, and . . . okay, my boyfriend.

But that wasn't quite true. *We'd* done it. All of us. Together.

I'd had my little piece in the form of the solo, but if it weren't for the group, I wouldn't be here in the first place. It wasn't about me, it was about the Hellcats.

Sure, it seems like a no-brainer, but ever since I had picked up my horn it had always been about me—my practice goals, my plans, my needs. And this was way, way bigger than that. Something finally clicked, and a rush of happiness flooded my body.

The band celebrated around me. I watched everyone's smiling faces, allowing myself to let it go, feeling waves of gratitude for them, feeling like I truly belonged.

41

By the time we boarded the bus to go home, I was feeling just as good as everyone else about our performance, and had even managed to accept a few compliments regarding the solo.

"You two," Mr. Sebastian directed at Steve and Punk as we made our way to the bus, "surrender any tools you have. NOW."

"*And*," I added, forcing a stern tone and trying to hide a grin, "I told you I had plans for you." They glanced at each other, uneasy. I was *so* not letting them off the hook for locking me in the bathroom. "I don't want you conspiring on the ride home. Hector, did you bring your *Star Wars* DVDs?"

He patted the outside pocket of his backpack. "Don't leave home without 'em."

I turned to Punk. "Switch seats with Sarah. You have to listen to Hector recite lines all the way home." Punk gave a theatrical sigh.

"What about my punishment?" Steve asked, acting tough. I glanced at Sarah, whose mouth was open in shock or delight—or maybe both.

"I'm sure Sarah can figure something out," I said, and grinned.

After that, I nearly crept into my seat on all fours. I was that tired.

"Unbelievable," Hector said from across the aisle.

"Totally," Jake agreed, appearing in the aisle. He'd helped load the equipment truck, and squeezed into the window seat next to me. Fairy fingers skittered across the back of my neck. "At least we'll have the rest of the weekend to recover."

"Not all of us." I groaned. "I have my audition in two days. And the director of Shining Birches witnessed my gak."

"Chicken," Punk said, "he'll never know it was you. Seriously. Let it go. You'll be *fine*."

I pretended to laugh with the others, but I was terrified. Would I be able to play? I'd felt so good about my pieces the other day, but now, who knew? My nerves were shot. What would this do to my confidence?

It was like Jake knew my thoughts. "You'll do great," he said, wrapping an arm around me. "You are the Zombie Chicken who survived the Bathroom of Doom and played to tell about it."

I laughed for real at his lame joke. "Maybe that's the

name I'll give to the audition panel," I said. "At least they'll know I'm not going down without a fight."

That started a whole conversation between Jake, Hector, and Punk about who would win in a fight—from me versus the audition panel to Han Solo versus Mr. Spock. I switched seats with Jake so he could speculate without leaning across me. I rested my head against the bus window, hand entwined with Jake's, replaying the events of the last few hours in my head, then thinking about the work I'd put into Shining Birches.

At least it'll be over soon, I thought, and finally drifted off to sleep.

I only wished I could've stayed that way. When we arrived at school, my parents—along with the rest of the town—were there to greet us, like we were celebrities or something. A local TV crew and a few reporters were camped out in the parking lot, waiting to interview the band about our experience.

Once they heard that I was the girl who'd been playing "that big trumpet solo," reporters surrounded me like hungry birds around stale bread.

"What's your name?" one called.

"So you play trumpet?" squalled another.

"Tell us how it felt to be on national television," peeped a third.

"Elsie Wyatt. It's a mellophone, not a trumpet. *Mel-lophone*. And it felt pretty awesome." What did they think I'd say, that I hated it?

While Mom prattled, I got my stuff and tried to avoid the reporters (I spotted Punk with a photographer, shooting his striped orange-and-black Hellcats hair). A news crew shot footage of Sarah and a few of the color guard doing spins and tosses.

Jake met me by the bus, holding my mellophone case.

"You're going to do great at that audition, you know," he said, handing it to me.

I smiled. "Thanks. For . . . lots of stuff."

He leaned over and gave me a quick kiss, with a promise to check in and see how everything went.

Dad found me a second later, a guarded smile on his face.

"You were wonderful," he told me. For once, I didn't care that he heard—or saw—me mess up.

"I want you to meet someone," I said to him. My heart was pounding, but I didn't feel as nervous as I would have even before we left. Things were different now. *I* was different now.

"Hey Jake," I called. He'd gone back to the luggage bay under the bus, and returned carrying his duffel bag. "I want you to meet my dad. Dad, this is Jake. He's . . ." I paused to find the right words. "He's important to me."

My dad extended his hand for Jake to shake.

"Elsie did an awesome job," Jake said. "I bet her chops are shot."

"Her mom and I are very proud," Dad responded, giving me a big smile.

I smiled back. Jake wished us a happy Thanksgiving and went back to help unload.

On our walk to the car, before Dad could say anything about Jake, or the botched solo, a woman flagged us down. She looked young and was carrying a notebook.

"Elsie—Ms. Wyatt—one more word. You must have worked hard for that solo. What does marching band mean to you?"

Okay, that stopped me in my tracks. Dad stepped on my heels.

Everything I'd realized during the parade flashed through my mind. Originally, I'd wanted to do a great job on the solo so my dad would see me on TV and . . . what? Think I was a good player? Take me seriously? I'd wanted him to realize that forever, and no Sousa solo was going to change his mind. Marching band was about *me*, not him.

I wanted to be on TV, playing that solo as best I could, because . . .

"I love this group," I answered. "And I'm proud of what we did today."

I smiled at the reporter and climbed in the car, not even glancing to see my dad's reaction.

42

That night, after I enjoyed some of Aunt Denise's dry reheated Thanksgiving turkey, my mom and I sat on the couch together and watched coverage of the parade on the news. The story began with a summary of the Minutemen's accident and even showed a grainy cell phone camera video of a piece of our performance at the competition. Then there was footage from the Darcy's parade.

We saw the Hellcats marching in to the parade review stand, color guard with their flags at a carry and the instrumentalists sharply at attention. Then it switched to us, mid-performance, as we broke into the marching maneuver just before my solo. They even showed me playing, close up. My eyes were closed, and the combination of intensity and joy on my face was hard to miss.

"Beautiful," Mom said.

"Absolutely," Dad agreed. I hadn't even realized he'd entered the room. Two days ago, I'd have been nervous and angry and all kinds of awful if he came in. Now I was fine.

The three of us watched the end of the segment—shots of our bus pulling into the school parking lot and us unloading, a brief interview with Mr. Sebastian and Punk ("It's all about band love," he said, in response to the question about his hair), and after a few pithy comments from the anchor—"not a turkey in the bunch," was one—it was over.

My mom clicked off the TV, shot Dad a very serious look over my head, and left. I picked at the fringed hem of the blanket draped over my lap. Dad sat on the end of the couch, in the same spot that Mom had vacated.

He leaned forward and rubbed his eyes under his glasses.

"I probably haven't done a good job of telling you this, Elsie, but I am really, really proud of all you've done this term. Starting high school is a big deal, and you not only balanced your new class load, but took on marching band as part of your audition package. It's impressive."

I considered his words. Hearing him finally say that he was proud of me was nice, but as I'd realized earlier, I didn't *need* him to say it. It was time to make decisions that were right for *me*. I could still be a professional horn player, still go to the New England Conservatory and travel around the world playing my instrument, still go to Shining Birches, even—but I didn't have to take every step that he did to get there. It was time to follow my own path. And stop hiding behind my horn to avoid anything hard or upsetting.

"Thanks," I said, not knowing how to explain my feelings.

"You stretched yourself taking that solo," he said. "It was brave. I respect that."

Okay, even if I didn't need him to say he was proud of me . . . hearing that I had his respect made me puff up with pride. After all, he *is* the principal horn player in the Boston Symphony Orchestra.

"The band needed me to play it," I explained, blushing. I couldn't stop myself. "I worked really hard."

"Honey, your dedication blows me away. I *know* how good you are, and how much work that takes. You don't have to hide that—every musician works hard. And it's awful when that hard work doesn't pay off. This is not an easy pursuit."

He was right. I *did* hide from him. I'd been shutting him out from the thing we both loved instead of sharing it with him because I was afraid he was judging me and that I'd come up short. Instead, all he wanted was to protect me. He was so afraid to let me grow up and face reality that he tried to keep me safe from everything—including, ironically, my horn.

"I'm not afraid of getting rejected, because I know how hard I've worked—and that's good enough for me," I said, finding confidence as I spoke. "And," I added, "I *love* marching band."

"I know you do," he said. "I've been so focused on my own experience that I didn't think there was value in doing things any other way. Music is about passion and heart and love, and if a group brings those feelings out in you, it's the right place *for* you."

The season flashed before me: learning a new instrument, dealing with the uniform, drilling eight to five steps, passing out, the field show competition and bleacher collapse, fighting with my parents in the parking lot, fighting with my friends all season, getting locked in the bathroom, the rise and fall of the solo, having Mr. Sebastian stay late and help me practice my pieces for the past two weeks—I'd done it all for Shining Birches.

At least, I *thought* it was for Shining Birches. Turns out, I'd learned a few things—how to be a good friend, how to be part of an extended family, how to support something larger than myself, and maybe even how to have a boyfriend—that had nothing to do with music but everything to do with heart and passion and joy. And marching band.

And if Dad hadn't brought us to Austria last spring, none of this would have happened.

This was a full-on "Ode to Joy" moment. I wrapped my arms around my dad and gave him a big squeeze.

He was right.

I'd found my place.

Coda

So, that Saturday, Dad and I drove to Chestnut College for my Shining Birches audition.

In spite of my insane Thanksgiving, I managed to get my nerves under control and played phenomenally well. It didn't hurt that I sat behind a screen during my audition, so I couldn't see the panel and they couldn't see me . . . or that I'd doused my slick palms with baby powder before picking up my instrument.

Later, I found out that Richard Dinglesby—Mr. "sit smack in the middle of the Darcy's review stand and throw off soloists" himself—praised my playing. When I met him at the post-audition reception he asked how my holiday had been. I proudly told him where I'd spent my Thanksgiving, fully expecting him to scoff at marching band, just like my dad.

"Wonderful!" he cheered. "I played trumpet in my high school and college marching bands. Best time of my life," he added. If he'd sprouted wings and flown out of the room, I wouldn't have been as shocked. We talked drill charts and field show music for fifteen minutes. I even admitted I was the Hellcats soloist.

And as for the audition . . .

I was the youngest person accepted into the program in over a decade.

I was the youngest person *ever* accepted on French horn.

But I'm not going. Not this summer, anyway.

Shining Birches' schedule interferes with band camp.

Acknowledgments

There's a whole ensemble that helps a book come together. I'd like to extend heartfelt thanks to:

My agent, Sally Harding, for her patience, responsiveness, and support. Thank you for believing in my work.

My lovely editor at Dial Books, Liz Waniewski, for her insight, thoughtfulness, and care with the manuscript, and thanks to the whole Dial team—copyeditor Regina Castillo for polishing my words, designers Linda McCarthy, Jeanine Henderson, and Nancy Leo-Kelly for making the book beautiful. I am so grateful for all of their efforts on this book's behalf.

My writing group: Annette, Gary, Heather, Megan, Ruthbea, and Phoebe, for their critiques of multiple drafts, support group services, and keeping me on track and focused.

The 2009 Debutante author's group, for their continued support, encouragement, and virtual chocolate. Extra-special thanks to Debs Jackson Pearce, for sharing color guard expertise, Saundra Mitchell, for the real-life chocolate, and Kate Messner, for providing space and time to write at the Swinger of Birches retreat.

Julie Berry, for coaxing, listening, and evaluating.

The friends and family who took the time to read various stages of the manuscript and help with technical details: Jerry Kazanjian, Katie Huha, and Bonnie Dougherty.

My daughter, who keeps me grounded, laughing, and constantly telling stories.

My husband, Frank—whom I wouldn't have met if it weren't for marching band—and who takes on roles of house elf, chef, therapist, primary dog walker and child care provider when I'm on a deadline . . . and does it all with patience and good humor.

The band directors whose programs were a venue for a bookish, shy girl to grow into a confident leader. Thank you, Mr. Jones and Mr. Miller, and special thanks to Sebastian Bonaiuto and Bob Mealey. The work you do reaches far beyond fields and stages.

And, last but not least, many, many thanks to everyone I marched with at Laguna Hills High School, Los Altos High School, and Boston College, including Katie Ginder-Vogel, Dan Johnson, Annie Watson, Bill Murray, Brad Davis, Shelagh Abate, Corrie Chomich Steeves, Amy Workman, Kayte Bellusci, Jeff Pelletier, Sarah Brenner, Jessica Madon, Chuck Keefe, Rick Laferriere, Sara Gibb, Bill Dougherty, Brian Nolan, Matt Kita, and Kara Fitzgerald. All of you look great in polyester.

Turn the page for a sneak peek at

Erin Dionne's laugh-out-loud novel

Chapter 1

"NO WAY," I hissed through the slatted dressing room door. "I am not coming out."

"Honey, I have to see how it fits," Mom said. "Let me look."

I dropped my forehead against the beige cubicle wall. I'd have to give in eventually, but I wasn't opening up until my cousin was back in the clothing cubby next to me.

"Oh, angel! It's just bee-yoo-ti-ful on you. Isn't she a sight, Noelle?" Aunt Doreen's nasal whine came over the top of my dressing room door like arrows over a castle wall. Of course the dress was "bee-yoo-ti-ful" on Kirsten. What wasn't? She was tall, blond, athletic, and one of the nicest people I knew. She also shared my celebrity crush on singer Theo Christmas. We both fell in love with him when her older sister took us to see him in concert last summer. I swear, he was singing to me the whole time. (She disagrees.)

"Does it look okay from the back?" Kirsten asked. I imagined her pirouetting in front of the three-way mirror at the end of the row, hair twirling like a shampoo commercial, evenly tanned skin standing out against the back of the dress, pastel lace and fabric hugging her in all the right places. I chose the only dressing room without a mirror on purpose.

"It's lovely," my mother offered, her voice tight. "Will you come *out?*" she stage-whispered through the dressing room door. "This is ridiculous."

"Where's Celeste?" Aunt Doreen said. "I haven't seen her yet. Celeste, do you need help in there?"

I cringed. "No, Auntie, I'm fine," I called. "Just, uh, almost ready. One more minute." I tugged at the dress, hoping for the magical yank that would straighten seams, smooth wrinkles, or snap it into the right proportion. Sometimes you don't need a mirror to know when things are *very* wrong.

"Kirsten, turn around again. I think it needs hemming, don't you?" Aunt Doreen said. "Let's get that seamstress in here." Then, louder, directed at me, "Okay, Celeste, we're waiting."

Ready or not, here I come, I thought. Sliding the door's bolt back, I hiked up the skirt and stepped into the dressing room corridor, head high. Maybe it wasn't as bad as it felt.

Aunt Doreen gasped, then covered her mouth as if to trap what might follow. I let the dress sag to the floor.

"It's . . . Oh, honey," Mom tried. "It needs some alterations."

I could imagine.

"Some?" said Aunt Doreen, biting the word like a potato chip. "What size did you order?"

I hung my head, trying to dampen the zing of her words,

2

trying not to hear Mom explaining that we needed to order an adult size because the youth sizes weren't cut for me. Besides, Mom said, a seamstress could fix it so the dress would "fall right," whatever that meant.

"Wait!" barked a short white-haired woman with a tape measure around her neck and a handful of pins. She stood in the doorway between the dressing rooms and the rest of Angelique's Bridal Boutique. "Don't move or you'll tear the lace!" When she said it, though, "move" came out like "moof" and "the" sounded like "ze." I stayed put. Besides, where could I go in a falling-wrong dress?

"Zis needs several substantial alterations," she said, gesturing in my direction with her chin. "When is the wedding?"

"Nine weeks," Mom said, tearing her eyes away from me and turning to the seamstress. "Can it be fixed in time?"

Straight out of a soap opera, I thought. *I'm in critical condition.* I stared at my feet, lost in a puddle of apricot satin. Usually I avoided this type of situation—comfort was more important to me than fashion. Comfort meant clothes that didn't pull, ride up, or show off too much. Comfort was soft, cozy, and worn; not lacy, satiny, or peachy. A movement caught my eye. Kirsten, the Barbie Bridesmaid, was slipping into her dressing room. She raised her perfectly shaped eyebrows in an expression of sympathy before closing the door.

A bony hand pushed against the small of my back, and the seamstress ushered me to the carpet-covered platform in front of the three-way mirror Kirsten had just vacated. I hoisted myself up and thought, *I hate Kathleen.*

3

Kathleen was the bride. She's Kirsten's older sister, my oldest cousin. Ever since we moved to Los Alvios, California, five years ago, she'd watched me and my brother, Ben, when my parents went out or away for the weekend. I was flattered that she asked me to be a junior bridesmaid in her wedding, but once I saw the Peach Monstrosity, I wondered if my parents owed her babysitting money.

The dress was designed for someone like Kirsten. It had two layers sewn together down the length of the side seams. The bottom layer was fitted at the chest, with thin spaghetti straps holding the flimsy satin in place. The narrow waist dropped into a skinny skirt with a high slit in one leg and a mermaid-like swoosh of fabric in the back. The other layer was frothy peach lace that followed the shape of the satin, except the top had a scoop neck with elbow-length sleeves and slightly tufted shoulders.

Standing in front of the mirrors, I saw just how substantial those alterations would have to be.

I'm what you call "chubby" if you're nice, "fat" if you're like Lively Carson at school. Mom and Dad say that I haven't lost my baby fat. If that's the case at thirteen, I must have a lot of growing left to do. I'm short and round in the middle. And the bottom. Basically, I'm round all over, just like my dad. According to the way the dress fit, though, I'd once been six feet tall and had suddenly turned into a watermelon.

The lace constricted my upper chest and arms, forcing my pale skin through the pattern's openings. Blood pressure cuffs make looser sleeves, and I could see a purple line around each forearm under the seams. The fabric hung loosely over my chest, bunched at my belly and hips, and puddled around my feet. And the view was reflected over and over in the triple mirror in front of me.

This is why I always shop for myself, I thought, trying to avoid the multiple Celestes. I settled on staring at a spot above my own head. Mom complains that I buy the same stuff all the time when I'm at the mall with Sandra, my best friend. She says that my wardrobe "makes me look like a lump" and that I am "hiding my beauty under hoods and zippers." It's true that my closet is home to track pants and hoodies in a range of colors, but I know what looks good on me. When Mom gets fed up with my clothes, she brings home outfits for me to try on. Then she gets fed up with my labeling them "too tight," "too uncomfortable," or "showing too much" and returns them. This dress definitely fit multiple "too *something*" categories.

"We can take extra fabric from the bottom to make the side panels," the seamstress muttered as she buzzed around my feet, measuring here and pinning there. "The lace sleeves will be a challenge."

"It's my daughter's wedding," said Aunt Doreen, her voice climbing. "You have to make it fit."

"Mom," Kirsten called from her dressing room, "can you help me get out of this?" After a moment's hesitation, Aunt Doreen huffed to her aid.

The coil of anxiety that had been growing in my chest loosened. *Thanks, Kirsten,* I thought. Aunt Doreen was seconds from going nuclear.

I caught my mother's eyes in the mirror. Mom's got great

eyes—toffee-colored, with tiny green flecks that sparkle when she's angry or happy. I got my dad's eyes, kind of. His are dark brown, deep like chocolate, but mine resemble mud. Mom offered a smile that was supposed to be encouraging. I tried to smile back.

Kirsten, out of her dress and into a pink tank and jeans, hustled Aunt Doreen from the changing rooms and into the rest of the store.

When "ze" seamstress inserted the final pin and I was free from my reflection, I shuffled to my dressing room and wriggled out of the Monstrosity and into the day's blue hoodie and track pants. I wrapped my hair into a knot, hoisted my bag, and tried to forget the peach watermelon in the mirror.

For more from Erin Dionne, check out

Available wherever books are sold!